Magnolia Weeping

Magnolia Weeping

A NOVEL

Lynn Roberson

WESTBOW
PRESS®
A DIVISION OF THOMAS NELSON
& ZONDERVAN

WestBow Press books may be ordered through booksellers or by contacting:

WestBow Press
A Division of Thomas Nelson & Zondervan
1663 Liberty Drive
Bloomington, IN 47403
www.westbowpress.com
1 (866) 928-1240

ISBN: 978-1-9736-7374-3 (sc)
ISBN: 978-1-9736-7373-6 (e)

Print information available on the last page.

WestBow Press rev. date: 11/5/2019

Part One

The afternoon light was fading as Iris stepped out of her boyfriend's car. She waved prettily to him, but he was looking over his shoulder, backing out of the driveway. Neither of them saw the tall, sleek man-shadow that slid across the porch wall, moving stealthily toward her.

Albert would be back in a couple of hours to drive her to her night job, she thought contentedly. She was turning to bounce into the house when she found herself snatched into the porch shadows—a large, hot hand clamped over her mouth. She struggled to free herself, but to no avail.

The man bent his face to whisper in her ear, "Keep your voice down. Don't make a sound."

The voice was not menacing. In fact, it sounded eerily familiar. The girl twisted her head to look into his face. Then she yanked his hand loose from her mouth.

"Reuben–??" she gasped aloud.

"Keep your *voice* down," he insisted.

She spun to fully face him. "—Reuben, it *is* you! Oh my! *Reuben!*"

"Listen to me, Sis—"

"Are you home to stay? Please say yes." Iris was beside herself, half-crying, half-laughing. "Does Mama know you're home?" she sniffled.

"Just wait. Be quiet and I'll tell you everything. Settle down, now, girl."

Reuben ran his hands nervously over his face. " I can't stay—and I can't rightly say why, so don't ask."

"What happened? Did you—did you break out of prison?" Iris whispered, resting a tentative hand on his arm.

"No. Nothing like that. I'm out legal—on parole."

"Honest?"

"Have I ever lied to you? But I'm still in some trouble. Not with the law—just with some guys. And if I hang around here, you'uns might be in trouble too. I can't take that chance."

Iris' face was ashen. She gazed into her brother's eyes, so dark brown and so restless. He was handsome, even though his face was dirty from travel and creased from worries he would not confide.

"Let me get Mama out here," Iris said, making a move away from him.

He caught her hand hastily. "Is Daddy still at the peach orchard? I got to be gone before he gets home."

"He's at work."

"What time does he get off?"

"Different times."

"Iris, he can't know I've been here."

"Mama's in the kitchen starting supper—but Reuben, whether you go in there or I call her out here, away from the kids, you *know* she'll tell Daddy. She tells him everything."

The young man's face clouded. His sister was right. He rubbed his eyes with both hands and exhaled a frustrated sigh. He didn't want his father yelling at Mama because he wasn't there himself to be yelled at.

The faint sound of a car in the distance, coming up the long country road toward the house, made them both freeze. But it made a detour and never passed their door. Reuben's tight shoulders sagged.

"I ought to just go," he muttered, making a reluctant move toward the forest that nearly surrounded their house.

"Don't go," his sister pleaded, tugging at his soiled sleeve. "It's so good to see you again, Reuben. Stay. Please?"

Iris had always been able to cajole her brother into doing anything she asked, ever since she was small. She reached up now and touched the side of his rough, unshaven face with the smooth palm of her hand. "You'll never guess what—I was thinking about you just yesterday!"

He smiled uneasily. "Thinking what?"

"I was remembering when we went down to the lake the last summer you were here. And you showed me how to skip rocks across the water."

He nodded, head bent. "Yeah, you got pretty good at that."

"You *do* remember," she said, pleased.

"I remember everything." His fleeting smile was gone and Iris' own smile faded with it.

"Don't. Please. Don't remember the bad times."

His gaze lowered to meet her upraised eyes. How this young girl used to catch hold of his heart with a simple glance! But all that was changed now.

"When I left, you were just a scrawny little thing. You've growed up beautiful," he said ambivalently.

"Well," she said, catching his tone. "Thank you—I guess. Is that a bad thing?"

"I just hate to think of some guy talking you into marrying—moving away from here, to who knows where. He'll have you cooking, washing, cleaning, and doing all the things married women are expected to do. He'll have you making babies all the time. You'll be wore out just like Mama."

"I'm not thinking about marrying," she assured him, with only partial honesty. "I'm too young for that yet."

"I saw you get out of that fella's car."

"That's Albert. We just got back from a matinee, and after supper he'll come and give me a ride to work."

"You got you a *job* now?" His eyes widened.

"Canady's Drug Store, downtown." Iris smiled. "Aren't you proud of me?"

His face was confused. "Well, I reckon—but—I thought you were still in high school."

"I have one more year to go."

"Inman High. Right?"

"I only work nights and some Saturdays."

He nodded thoughtfully. "Girl, what*ever* you do, don't quit school. I did and then I got into trouble from all sides."

"Oh, I'm gonna graduate. Don't you worry."

Reuben took her hand in his and helped her sit down on the edge of the porch, in a corner hidden by the shadows of the trees.

"Tell me everything, Iris," he said, just above a whisper. "Start with our little brothers and Maggie. No, start with Mama. Is she doing all right?"

"Yeah, she's okay. You've been gone—what—four years?"

He nodded.

"She worries about Maggie."

Reuben put his hands together and cracked his knuckles. Then he bounced his sister's hand lightly in his own, deep in thought.

"You know, Iris, something ain't right with Maggie."

"I know," came a small whisper. "But I don't want to talk about that right now. I've got you for such a little while."

"Just watch out for her, will you?"

"Always have and always will."

"So what *would* you like to talk about then?"

"Well, Nathan is almost six. He's the baby and it shows. Jackson is thirteen and he's an artist. He draws real-life pictures, you ought to see them! I bet if he had better paper and things he could sell them. He just uses notebook paper."

"Can't somebody get him some drawing paper?"

"Money is tight."

"Maybe I can get him some."

"How you gonna do that? You get rich in prison?" Iris gave him a playful nudge.

"Hey—" Reuben smiled. "What's the good of being an ex-con if you can't put a five-finger-discount on a pad of drawing paper?"

"Don't even joke about that," Iris scolded.

"I saw Sonny in Columbia," he replied, changing the subject. "He was making deliveries at a place where I was working a temp job. Man, was I surprised to see him!"

"No more than he was, I'm betting."

"It was real good," Reuben admitted. "It was. He never mentioned prison or anything. He just talked about his long haul driving. He drives a big rig now."

"Yep. Daddy's crazy proud of him. My little part-time job doesn't count I guess."

"Why do you reckon—well, why do you reckon Mama and Daddy went and had six children?" Reuben fretted.

Iris blushed. "Sometimes babies just come along."

"Yeah, they sure do. I wish I could see Mama."

Iris rubbed the back of his hand with one finger. "Say the word. I'll go fetch her."

Reuben considered this. "But she'd tell him for sure?"

"You know as well as I do."

He sighed. "You know, having six kids—looks like they'd know to expect one bad apple."

"I hope you're not referring to yourself." Iris pouted prettily.

"Well, I'm sure not talking about you," he grinned, bumping his shoulder against her own. "Naw, seriously. I'm trouble, and you know it."

Iris did know it. "Are you trying to escape the draft? Are you afraid you'll get sent to Vietnam? Is that why you're sneaking around?"

The young man shook his head quietly. "I just got to find a place to land, Sis. Start my life over. And it can't be here."

"Maybe it could—if you talk to Daddy—"

"Daddy don't want to see my face *ever again*. He done told me so, after the trial, when they were taking me away."

Iris's eyelashes lowered, covering her eyes. She couldn't face him in the light of this new information. She leaned her head against his shoulder.

"Well, I want you to stay," she murmured at last. "It's been a long, long time. Maybe he's eased up some."

"Daddy?" Reuben gave a low, harsh laugh. Then he softened and put an arm around her. "It's real good to see you, though. Will you do something for me?—will you give Mama a hug for me sometimes? Don't even tell her, just do it?" He averted his face.

"I will," the girl promised. "Sure."

In the twilight he swallowed hard, almost convulsively. His sister saw.

"Oh, Reuben," she murmured, grieved. Again she pulled at his shirt sleeve, but this time he pulled away and stood up.

In the distance another car was coming up the road. Before Iris could say anything else, Reuben had slipped into the shadows of the nearby woods and was lost to sight.

Sadly, Iris went inside.

Martha Burnett sat at her kitchen table in a rare moment of solitude, snapping string beans for supper.

She smiled as Iris stooped to kiss her cheek.

"Good movie?" she asked perfunctorily.

"Yes ma'am," Iris said, climbing upstairs to her bedroom. She didn't trust herself to chat with Mama. She would be sure to let it slip about Reuben.

Martha's thoughts wandered, touching on each of her children in turn. Absently, she reached into her apron pocket and fingered the edge of the troubling document hidden there. Maggie, her ten year old, was doing poorly as ever in school. The familiar worry turned her thoughts yet again to her young adult son, Reuben, who had also found school difficult and frustrating. At the last, he had dropped out. Now he was four years gone with no communication.

She thought of Reuben too much, she chided herself. He was a man when he made the choices that led to separation from his family. Yet she could not free herself from reliving the persistent middle-of-the-night knock on their door—the trepidation as her husband Lester answered—the somber look on the policeman's face. The words, "Your son has been arrested as an accessory in an armed robbery."

From that night, by Lester's decree, the family was forbidden to talk about Reuben or even speak his name.

But the troubled young man was remembered daily in the silence of his mother's aching and anxious prayers.

Martha had noticed of late that Maggie reminded her of Reuben. Vague, ephemeral resemblances impossible to put into words. They were both gentle souls most of the time. They both preferred not to mix too much with other people. Neither was inclined to chatter the way her other children did. Neither was successful in school. Both had a peculiar way of tugging at her heart.

The thought of schoolwork drew her hand back to her pocket. Yesterday, June second, had been the final day of school, the beginning of summer vacation. She had emptied the younger children's book bags only to find an overdue library book with a belated report card tucked between the pages.

Her mind was filled with anxious questions.

Martha's younger children, oblivious to her worry, were intoxicated with the sudden freedom of summer. Martha had not yet found sufficient chores to keep them busy for more than a few hours. Now the front screen door banged and Jackson, not yet fourteen, came barreling into the house.

"No running in the house," Martha called out to him.

The boy appeared in the doorway of the kitchen.

"Hey, Mama."

"What you got there, boy?"

Jackson was holding a his school notebook under his arm. "It's a picture of a flower I drew. For you," he added shyly.

"Let's have a look," she murmured pleasantly, without ceasing to string the beans.

"Here. I can show you what I got so far." Jackson crossed the kitchen and came back with the bloom in a shallow bowl of water. He carried the bowl carefully in both hands and set it on the table in front of his mother. "This here is what I copied it from," he explained.

Martha nodded. "That's a magnolia."

Next he opened his notebook and showed Martha the drawing: gracefully sweeping curved lines and waxy curling petals, gently shaded in grey pencil.

"Oh, my," she said, casting him a smile. "It looks so real. You did good, son."

"But something's wrong," Jackson fretted. "I picked it off the tree yesterday, and I've kept the stem in water—but when I got up this morning, it wasn't white anymore. It had turned a sandy looking color—kind of—light brown. And the petals were drooping."

Martha put a light hand on her son's shoulder. "They don't keep long at all," she confirmed. "Even in water. It's just the nature of magnolias. But the leaves will stay glossy and green for a long time. And leaves are pretty, too."

"But look. It's leaking. Or dripping—nectar or something. From the center. See?"

She bent to look more closely.

"Well, I declare," she murmured.

"It looks like it's crying, Mama."

"Well, it kinda does look that way, for a fact. See there—that looks just like a tear running down a child's face."

Together they studied the drop on the stained petal and Jackson sighed heavily. "I ruined it, Mama. I didn't mean to do that. It was so pretty on the tree. I never should have picked it."

"Son, you're making way too much out of this. It's just a flower. They don't live very long. Especially magnolias." She took the notebook from his hand and propped it up on the counter top where it could be seen. "Your drawing is real pretty."

"I made it for you," Jackson reiterated, but his eyes were troubled.

Martha gave his hair a tousle. "Thank you. I like it. A lot." Then, changing the subject in the same breath, she inquired, "Have you seen your little sister?"

"She went off to play down in the woods back of the house."

"Well, she's been gone a right long time. Would you go fetch her for me? Make sure she gets home all right?"

"Sure, Mama. I'm on it. I know exactly where to look."

He bounded out the back door, not lingering to hear his mother add, "When you get back, Jackson, we need to talk."

Absently, she resumed snapping beans. Her heart would not be restful until her younger daughter was safely inside the house. The other children—even Nathan, her youngest—would meander in at mealtime. But Maggie—she was different. She always needed a reminder, a little more time, a deeper portion of patience. And protection.

Martha glanced at the clock, her fingers again worrying the edge of the card in her pocket.

A cooling breeze found its way in through the open kitchen window. Martha looked out to see the sky beginning to pink. "Lord," she whispered in near silence, "please keep my children safe and sound."

Usually this small prayer quieted her mind. Not so, today. There was a sense of something unsettled. A disturbance in her heart.

The child, Maggie, knelt by the creek, her bare knees pressed deep into the slick brown mud. A large tea strainer dripping creek water was clasped tightly in her fist. Her whole body was rigid, waiting, watching.

The surface of the water, moments ago green, shone darkly now, catching the bronzed light of a weary sun. Dusk had a way of crouching at the edge of these woods, biding its time, drawing out a thousand shadows perilously thin before abruptly casting its cloak of night.

Maggie watched as tiny, darting slivers of shadow grew thick in the shallow pool at her knees. She held herself steady. At the least sign of movement, the delicate gathering of minnows would shatter like glass. This she had learned well in the past hour.

So she waited, watching, until her shoulders ached from holding still, and the water had turned the color of burnished copper. The quivering shadows were now as thick as fruit flies on a day-old watermelon rind in July.

In a single, desperate gesture, she plunged the strainer into the creek and out again. She peered into the hollow of it expectantly.

But nothing.

Maggie sat back on her heels with a small sigh, sore shoulders drooping.

"Maggie, what are you doing?—"

Her brother's voice startled her visibly. In her concentration, she had not heard him making his way through the woods to find her. Her gaze leapt up like the eyes of a frightened fawn. The dark pupils shrank before the brightness of the late afternoon sun, until only her soft grey-blue irises were visible.

The boy, standing on the other side of the creek, facing her, seemed taller than he was; a towering silhouette against the sunset.

"You scared me, Jackson," his sister complained.

"Aw, don't be such a fraidy-cat." His voice came out in the uncertain tenor of a boy half-past thirteen. "What you doing, anyhow?"

"Catching minnows."

"What minnows," he said skeptically.

Maggie made no reply. A new tactic had suddenly occurred to her. She lowered the strainer gently into the water and held it flawlessly still—ready, this time, armed with fresh hope.

Jackson grinned. He stood watching, arms akimbo, his thumbs hooked in the side pockets of his overalls. All thoughts of the pale brown magnolia flower were gone. "Tell me this, then. Does Mama know you're down here scrapin' up the creek bed with her tea strainer?"

"I'll wash it," the girl said mildly.

Jackson squatted down and studied the golden surface of the water. He shook the strands of dark brown hair back from his eyes with a frown. His features were clear-cut and intelligent, with a light scattering of freckles across his nose that seemed out of place beneath his dark locks. "Where's these minnows you talking about? I don't see none."

"They're down there all right," she solemnly pronounced.

"Okay, so how many have you caught already? So far?"

"The thing is," she answered him, staring wistfully into the water, "they're awful quick—"

The boy let out a whoop of derisive laughter. Jackson had a hair-trigger sense of humor and couldn't help himself. But when his sister raised her solemn grey-blue eyes, puzzled and a little hurt by his laughter, he was instantly ashamed and sorry.

With a careful, practiced leap he crossed the small creek and stood at her side.

"Fact is, minnows are some of the quickest-moving critters around," he told her in consolation. "When they swim off, you don't see nothin', not even a blur hardly. They're just gone."

Maggie reluctantly nodded agreement.

"Listen here," he said quietly. "Never mind these minnows. I'll take you fishing for real one morning. Down where the creek water's deep and there's crappie and brim. Catfish, too. We'll bring us a pole and bait, and catch some real fish that Mama can cook for supper."

His mention of their mother reminded Jackson of his mission in coming there.

"Oh, yeah—Mama sent me to fetch you home. She's gettin' worried about you bein' gone so long."

Maggie gave him an uncomprehending look.

Jackson shrugged. "Mama worries."

The girl withdrew the dripping strainer, giving it a half-hearted shake. The droplets splattered the creek water like a shower of rain. Maggie watched them, brushing her unkempt yellow bangs out of her eyes with a muddy hand.

To Jackson she looked thin and small, even younger than her meager ten years, in the flour-sack dress handed down from their older sister, Iris. The dress was shapeless from too many washing; its tiny calico print had been bleached colorless by hours of hanging in the sun to dry.

"I want real fish," Maggie explained patiently to her brother, ignoring his last remark. "In a bowl. To be my friends."

"You can't make friends out of fish, Maggie. Leastwise, not minnows."

She turned her eyes to his without expression.

"Never mind," Jackson sighed. "Come on." He jumped lightly back across the creek.

Maggie put her bare right foot on the dry mud, matted with grass, and pushed upward. The slippery mud sucked at her left foot, trying to draw her back. Jackson caught her wrist, yanked her feather-light body clear into the air and set her down on clean grass. He turned and led the way along the narrow forest path towards home.

The path meandered between tall oaks, pines, and tangled wild grapevines. On either side, the forest floor was rich with ferns, mushrooms, moss, and every kind of wild foliage. The pungent fragrance of wet green leaves, black earth and pure air stung their nostrils lightly.

Jackson walked in front, his hands pushed down in the pockets of his faded blue overalls, his hard brown shoes ruthlessly kicking aside the arched fronds of ferns that had overgrown the path. He talked over his shoulder, trying to teach his sister—not for the first time—how to distinguish poison ivy from Virginia Creeper, and from the wild blackberry leaves with their ragged edges.

Maggie didn't listen. Her thoughts were vaguely absorbed in the varying shades of green she saw all around her. Brown-green burrows half-hidden in black-green shadows. Fern-green and pine-green, and the path dappled golden-green with sunlight.

At this time of day, the woods filled up with sound—frogs young and old, tuneful birds, things rustling and unseen. And, soaring above all the other noises, the poignant, sustained shrilling of the cicada—which in Maggie's mind was the most beautiful, and the loneliest, sound in all the world.

It was beginning to be dusk, now.

The cicada fell momentarily silent.

Vaguely Maggie became aware of her brother's voice, a good ten yards ahead, calling to her in a loud whisper. She looked up.

Jackson was standing at the edge of the path, trying to push aside the overgrown kudzu vine. Kudzu was rampant in the woods of South Carolina. Its thick leaves grasped back at him like pale green hands, open-palmed, too many to count. He squinted his eyes in vain, searching for something.

Maggie ran to catch up with him. "What?" she whispered. Her shoulder shoved against his arm in her eagerness to see.

"Quit pushing," he complained. "And don't stand so close. There's a big old snake in there, that's what. I saw the tail end of it for a split second, slithering across the path. Now it's hid."

Maggie shivered. She stood pressed against Jackson's arm. Gingerly he took firmer hold of the kudzu vine and spread the leaves apart. His eyes strained to see into the semi-darkness beneath.

"It's gone," he murmured, plainly disappointed. The next instant he stiffened. "No, it ain't," he whispered hoarsely. "Right there's its mid-section, sure as the world."

"I want to see," Maggie whispered urgently. But Jackson wouldn't step aside to let her in.

"You better stay back," he warned. "You ain't got shoes on, or nothing. And quit *pushing* on me!" he added severely. He looked into the green shadows, frowning. "Aw, I can't tell. The light's too dim, and there's leaves all in the way. Might be just a tree root. Too big around for a snake, now that I think on it."

"I could tell."

"No, you couldn't." Jackson looked around behind him, still holding the vines in both hands. "Hand me that stick there."

"What for?" she wanted to know.

He scowled. "Just do it. And don't take half-a-forever about it."

Maggie brought the stick and held it out to him, pushing her uneven bangs out of her face with her other hand.

"Okay," Jackson said, nodding toward his right hand. "Take this vine here and hold it up, same as I been doing. Got it?"

She nodded.

The boy stooped down, still holding the kudzu vine with his left hand.

"Easy now," he cautioned, speaking to himself in a smooth whisper. He gave the questionable tree root a tentative poke with the stick.

Quicker than lightning—with a sound like rushing wind—the snake sprang into a coil!

The kudzu leaves burst apart, shattered by a huge, dark-scaled head—fangs glistening, red tongue leaping out like a quivering streak of living fire.

Maggie had time to let out only a fraction of a scream before Jackson shoved her furiously back, away from the kudzu. She lost her footing and tumbled backward onto the dirt path.

For an instant Jackson stood transfixed, clutching the stick, now, like a weapon. He could not think what to do. The snake remained poised, its enormous head weaving ever so slightly, piercing eyes fixed on its mark.

The snake and the boy struck at the same instant. In the sudden, wild confusion of the moment, neither one's aim proved true. But Jackson's wits returned.

In a single blur of motion he threw the stick wildly into the kudzu, snatched Maggie to her feet, and took off at a dead run for the house.

Maggie shut her eyes and ran on bruised bare feet, clutching her brother's hand and stumbling along behind him like a blind child.

By unspoken agreement, Maggie and Jackson stopped where the edge of the woods met the bare dirt clearing of their own back yard.

They listened, breathless. Behind them all was quiet.

They were safe, now, and they rested, panting, their eyes turned hungrily to the light of home.

The old house was almost beautiful in the dusk, its every flaw forgiven by the dim twilight.

In the bright light of day, viewed from the back, where the children now stood, the house's need of repair showed badly—the grey, weathered boards, with remnants of peeling paint, porch screens torn and bulging out between their frames. The steps were sagging, propped up with cinder blocks. Two upper story windows, long broken, were covered by ragged sheets of cloudy plastic stapled to the window frames. In the harsh reality of day, the house looked old and neglected.

But tonight it was a grand, strong shadow against the dusk. Golden light streamed through its windows like arms stretched into the coming darkness, drawing its children safely home.

Maggie and Jackson, in one accord, took off running across the wide, bare dirt backyard, in a race to the porch.

Jackson reached their destination first and slammed his hand against the back door frame.

"Winner!" he yelled over his shoulder to Maggie.

She slowed to a relaxed trot. "Well, you had shoes on and I didn't."

"Whose fault is that?"

Their little brother Nathan, almost six years old, was sitting on the porch steps, sucking on a dripping piece of ice.

"What you got, Nathan?" Maggie asked, arriving at the steps. She leaned in close with the urgency of combined curiosity and thirst. Sometimes their mother froze orange juice for them, in her aluminum ice cube tray. "Is that a juice-pop you got, Nate? Say." If there were any popsicles made, Maggie wanted one.

The little boy nodded indifferently.

Jackson bent down, squinting his eyes in the deep twilight, to see. "Is not," he scoffed. "It's nothing but a plain ice cube."

Nathan· was unperturbed. He clutched the ice in reddened fingers, slurping it contentedly.

Jackson plopped down on the step beside the boy and folded his arms across his knees.

"Nate," he began, in a low voice calculated to arouse curiosity. "What do you reckon Maggie and me saw down in the woods just now? Two guesses."

Nathan raised clear blue eyes to his brother's face. "A bear," he said without hesitation.

Jackson grimaced. "There's no bears in these woods, Nate! Use your head, for crying out loud! Go on, guess again."

But Nathan's feelings were hurt. He shook his head no, and slurped his diminishing scrap of ice.

Jackson rolled his eyes, exasperated. "I'll tell you, then. It was the biggest, and the ugliest, and the meanest snake you ever saw in your whole life. A big old monster-snake, with a lizardy face, and a tongue flung out and flappin' red as a second-place ribbon at the fairgrounds. Wasn't it, Maggie?"

Maggie nodded soberly. "It was big," she agreed.

Jackson rolled his eyes. "Big? It was enormous—it was gigantic!"

Nathan looked from one to the other, with perfect indifference.

Maggie turned her eyes to her older brother's face. "You said a bad word," she informed him.

He frowned. "Did not."

"Did, too."

"What word? When?"

"When that snake hopped up and stuck out his tongue at us."

Jackson stared at her for a disbelieving second and then let out a whoop. "Hopped up? Snakes don't hop, Magsie, they strike, for heaven's sake—"

Jackson had a sudden, vivid image in his mind of that huge snake hopping along the path on the tip of its tail. He was instantly delirious with laughter.

"Well, I heard what you said," Maggie repeated. "And if I tell Mama she'll wash your mouth with soap."

Jackson's laughter choked down to breathless gasps. "Will not," he managed.

"She will too. You watch." Maggie started up the steps to the screen door, but Jackson caught her around the waist and pulled her back.

"You better mind your own business," he warned, and set her down lightly on the bare ground at the foot of the steps.

"Say you're sorry, then."

"'Bout what?"

"For what you said when—when—" she stopped there.

A crooked grin eased up one side of Jackson's face. He saw the opportunity for poking fun and snatched it. "What—when that snake hopped up at me? Is that what you're talking about?" He grinned condescendingly.

Maggie's face was sober.

She wasn't going to allow him any fun over this if she could help it, Jackson saw. He tried a new tactic. "Hey—" he said with mock innocence. "How can I apologize, when I can't remember what I said? What exactly was it, Maggie?" He leaned forward, bringing his face as close as possible in front of hers, unable to repress a small grin. "What word exactly did you hear me say, huh?"

Maggie's lips pouted. She wouldn't look at him.

"Hah," he exclaimed, triumphantly.

Nathan peered up into his sister's face. "Maggie's fixin' to cry," he announced wetly, his tongue pressed against the remaining sliver of melting ice.

Jackson's face fell into a frown. "She is not—you're lying," he said belligerently to the little boy.

Nevertheless, he laid an awkward hand on his sister's thin shoulder. "Mags?" he said tentatively. "You know I was only teasing, don't you?"

She brushed her hand against the corner of her eye, leaning her shoulder away from him.

He went on, "Hey, I'm sorry, okay? That ugly old snake just brought out the devil in me, somehow. I didn't mean to hurt your feelings, Maggie. That's the truth."

Maggie thought this over for a minute. She drew a shivering little breath and murmured, "I wasn't really gonna tell Mama."

"I know that," Jackson said soothingly, although he hadn't been any too sure.

He sighed, peering thoughtfully in the direction of the woods. "Hateful snake. I don't mind a little harmless kind of garden snake or something, they don't bother me for one second. But a rattler or a water moccasin—or one so way BIG like that one yonder—gives me the shivers."

Jackson sat down again on the step and gazed meditatively out over the thick woods. "I just hope it heads on down to the creek," he muttered. "That's all. I hope it don't take a notion to come up this way, towards the house."

Young Nathan stared up at his brother's face. The last bit of ice slid from his fingers and fell into the dust at his feet.

Maggie, only half-listening, was stepping onto the porch step and back down again, over and over, in a self-absorbed ritual of her own invention. She gave the two boys a disinterested glance, without breaking her rhythm.

"If it wasn't already mostly dark," Jackson mumbled to himself, "I'd get Daddy's gun and go back down there, while I know whereabout that snake's at—and I'd kill it. Kill it deader'n this here old chunk of brick." He gave the cinder block at his feet a contemptuous backward kick with his heel.

"You better not," Nathan piped up soberly. "Daddy said if—"

"Just hush up, Nathan," Jackson grumbled mildly. "I don't need you to tell me what I already know."

He leaned his head glumly against the porch post, staring toward the black-shadowed woods. "By now, that snake's liable to be a half-mile away from where we seen him, anyhow. Truth is, he could be anywhere by now."

Nathan peered across the backyard into the deep thicket of woods behind the house.

The rising moon, nearly full, cast eerie shadows—long, thin shadows that wriggled and writhed with every passing breeze.

"Snakes don't come 'round houses," the little boy haughtily declared, at the same time casting a worried glance toward his older brother.

"Who says they don't?" Jackson returned. "Sometimes they turn up right smack inside somebody's house. It happens."

"How?" Nathan demanded. "Snakes can't go up stairs. Can they?"

Jackson had not the least idea whether snakes could crawl up stairs or not. But he was not about to admit this to his younger brother.

He said, "'Course they can. Stairs ain't nothing to a snake. Don't you know anything? They can get anywhere they make up their mind to get."

Maggie crooked her arm around the porch post and swung herself down, landing at her brother's feet.

"You ought not to say—"

"Maggie, don't start," the boy told her wearily.

"I'm going in," she announced, picking up the tea strainer.

"Me, too," Nathan said, hurrying after her.

Jackson lingered, staring ruefully toward the woods a moment or two longer, before reluctantly following.

Lanky young Reuben lay on a mold-spattered cot in an abandoned cabin in the forest behind his home. The windows had no glass. There was no plumbing. The whole cabin smelled like wet ashes, black and sloppy. Reuben considered it an appropriate lodging for himself now.

No one was going to hire him after he had served time. Even though he was out free and clear on parole. Not in the South. And he was born a Southern boy.

He hadn't even finished high school. He couldn't imagine how to begin looking for a job. He could pick peaches, but then he would surely run into his father, Lester.

"I don't never want to see your face again." The words ached in his head, throbbing.

Reuben rubbed his brow with a vengeance and coughed. As if reminded by the cough, he dug in his worn shirt pocket and pulled out a fresh cigarette. But he didn't light it.

It had been good to see Iris. She really wanted him to stay. If it had been up to her he would. But it wasn't up to her, it wasn't even up to Mama. And Reuben had lost all courage to dare anything.

He gritted his teeth. Remembered beatings. But he was a grown man now. His father could not discipline him anymore. It would be an out and out fight between two men. And he knew he would win. He had grown strong in prison.

But that was not the issue. It was his father's face that terrified Reuben. And his mother's face if he dared to throw a punch in his own defense. There was no more home for him. No safe place.

A broken twig made Reuben jump visibly.

"Who's there?" he demanded.

"Just me," his friend Bo answered, bowing slightly to fit through the small doorway. "Don't have a stroke, man."

He stood just inside the door frame, eyeing Reuben with a dubious expression.

Bo was the same age as Reuben. He had dark red hair and green eyes. His handsome face, had it not been so menacing, looked like a Christmas ornament. This whimsical thought crossed Reuben's mind as he watched Bo sidle into the cabin.

"Like to never found you," Bo grumbled.

"Maybe I wasn't looking to be found."

"If I didn't know no better, I'd think you're not glad to see me, Bro."

"Don't call me that. I got three brothers, and you ain't none of 'em."

Bo chuckled malevolently. "I'm the friend that sticks closer than a brother," he declared.

Reuben looked away from him, disgusted. "Don't you ever listen? I told you *don't go following* me. I don't want you hanging around me anymore. What part of that do you not understand, anyhow? You're the reason I got in trouble in the first place, Bo. I know we were buddies in school—and then in the joint, but—" Reuben raised a hand for silence as Bo began to break in. "—I'm going it on my own, whatever happens. I can't change the past, but I can be clean from now on."

Bo rolled his eyes contemptuously around the filthy one room cabin strewn with spider webs, dust balls, rags and grit.

"Clean. Yeah, you're *clean* all right. Come on, Rube, don't be so stubborn. Kobra has paid all your parole fees. You owe him big time."

There was a pause in which no words were spoken. Reuben sat down on the cot with a sigh. He couldn't deny that he was indebted to their gang leader.

Then Bo continued in a friendlier tone: "You're one of the gang now, and hey, that's not so bad. We take care of each other. We got each other's back." He waited but Reuben refused to speak. "Hey, Rube, I can get you some fresh clothes—we're about the same size and build."

"No. I got to make it on my own."

"And food—I know you gotta be starving and sick to death of fish. How'd you like a nice thick steak and a baked potato. I can get it for you. No problem."

Reuben appeared to be considering this offer. "If you got a couple of cigarettes, I'll take those," he relented. "This is my last one." He held up the cold cigarette which was still in his hand.

Bo handed him an almost full pack. Reuben started to take one out.

"No, keep 'em. I can get more. I can get you just about anything you might need. But, Reuben, you got to be a team player."

Reuben handed the whole pack of cigarettes back. "No deal, man."

"How are you getting your meals? You're thinner than you was in the lock-up. You getting food from your kin folk? They live around here?"

"No—nowhere near," Reuben snapped back, making Bo's face smooth into arrogant comprehension.

"Oh. Is that a fact," he purred.

"Listen, you don't know where my family lives and you *better* make sure it stays that way. If you ever think you've maybe come up on my family's house you better run the other way, 'cause I *will* kill you."

Bo laughed out loud.

"And just what do you think is so funny?"

"You don't even have a gun," Bo smiled.

"Wouldn't need no gun," Reuben shot back with narrowed eyes.

A very awkward silence followed. No one seemed willing to break it. The two men faced away from each other.

In a matter of fact tone, Bo began again. "We have some hits in the works. Serious money. No more little liquor stores for us. But we need your help, Reuben."

Reuben remained stonily silent.

"What do you not understand about being a team player? We meet up, play cards, drink cold beer and make plans. We have fun. Once in a while we get rich. What about that do you not like?" The silence only thickened.

27

"Am I wasting my time here?" Bo asked mildly. "If I am, I'll just go for now. But I don't know what Kobra's going to say about the money you owe him. It's not over."

"It *is* over."

Bo shrugged. "Well. Guess I'll check you later," he said casually.

"I will take those cigarettes," Reuben said, suddenly remembering, "if you're still offering them."

"Why, you know it!" Bo handed over the nearly untouched pack. "Enjoy."

He stretched his long body until his hands touched the ceiling of the tiny cabin. "Ugh." He wiped the cobwebs on a torn dishrag lying on the table. But his hands wouldn't come clean to his satisfaction. He brushed them off on his own clothes, shuddering. Then, with a smooth salute, he slid out the open door and disappeared into the woods.

Martha had been preparing supper all this time. She wiped her perspiration-beaded forehead with the back of her left arm. With her right hand she stirred beans in a messy stock pot. The soup from the beans had already foamed over the top twice. The smell of burning broth was hot and rancid.

Her eyes glanced fretfully toward the window in the big, nearly barren living room, making sure it was fully open. Short, sheer curtains billowed in and out—curtains that had been there since her husband's great-grandmother was matron of this ancient, two-story house in the woods beyond

Gramling. That had been in the eighteen-hundreds, she reckoned. And here it was, summer of 1962, with no repairs or painting done since.

It must have been a beautiful house back then, she considered, picturing it in her mind—brilliant white, with a manicured lawn, and carefully tended flower beds. Lester's ancestors had owned a peach farm, and for decades they were wealthy. But three years of poor yield, from frost and hail damage, and the farm could not pay back the investment it had made in anticipation of a good crop. The family tried to sell the orchard and the business, all without luck. They were faced with inevitable foreclosure, and the farm was auctioned off to new owners—strangers.

Owning an orchard and working as hired help for a peach farmer were two very different things. As a peach flat driver, maintenance worker, and general handyman, Lester worked long hours and brought home little more than a few dollars a day. Occasionally the machines broke down several times in one day; and in the interim the peach shed workers were required to wait, but did not receive any pay for their time. It was a hard life for shed workers and pickers alike. But when the bushels had been packed and the ringers had arranged the top layer in perfect concentric circles and proudly attached the labels, there was a sense of undeniable satisfaction.

Martha had been one of the young girls working in the shed during spring and summers. She remembered once or twice starting bright and early at nine, and getting home at one the next morning. She worked alongside her aunt, who held the coveted position of a ringer. Men were not allowed in the sheds, generally. But sometimes she got a glimpse of young Lester driving the peach flat. Even then she had known she loved him.

Martha turned down the flame under the beans and sat in one of the kitchen chairs, allowing herself a moment's rest at the table.

She remembered the beauty of spring when she was a girl growing up in Inman—the many seemingly endless orchards were covered in fluffy pink blossoms as sweet-promising as spun sugar. How magical they had been in full spring bloom! And after the flowers there had grown enormous, perfect peaches. South Carolina peaches had been famous all across the nation for their excellence.

Opening her eyes brought her back to reality. She surveyed the visible portion of the house which had been inherited by Lester. In the livingroom—once a parlor—there was only an overstuffed chair, a faded, sunken sofa, and one floor lamp. And an old curio cabinet in the corner. The hardwood floors were bare and the room seemed huge and empty. In the kitchen were the long wooden table and almost a dozen simple ladder-back chairs with hand-woven rush seats.

Martha stood again and opened the oven door, making the room a few degrees hotter. Quickly she shut the door and turned the heat off. The cornbread was puffy and golden, with the lightest imaginable crust.

She allowed herself a small, brief smile of accomplishment. But in the next moment grease began popping like gunshots out of the over-heated pan she used to fry fatback. The grease splattered and burned her as she hurriedly turned down the heat and placed a lid on the pan.

With experienced proficiency, she quickly smeared yellow mustard on her hand and forearm; this unlikely home remedy, she had learned, soothed the pain and prevented blistering. Her brief smile was gone as she sat back down in one of the creaky rush-bottomed chairs to let her skin cool a minute before she returned to making dinner.

She wondered about Lester's ancestors. She imagined Mae Burnett assisted by servants. A familiar bitterness came over her. Mae's life would not have been dull and exhausting. She surely had her own cook and nanny. And, of course, maids to clean house. It made Martha vaguely sick to think of it.

"Jealousy," she murmured in less than a whisper. "Nothing but plain evil jealousy. Lord, Lord. Help me." She burrowed her forehead on her clean arm and fought away the tears that threatened. The vague, uneasy premonition of trouble swept over her again.

Martha had already searched every drawer in the kitchen for her tea strainer.

The tea was made, sitting in a three-quart pot beside the stove, cooling, with the leaves forming a murky, bitter sediment in the bottom of the pan.

When she heard the children coming in, she got up quickly, wiping the slight trace of tears off her face, and smoothing cool water over her arm, eradicating all signs of the mustard. Upon looking around, she saw the strainer in Maggie's hand. She sighed with mingled annoyance and relief.

"Maggie Burnett," she declared. "You know better than to take things out of their place without asking."

The displeasure in her mother's voice struck the little girl dumb. She stared at the floor in guilty silence.

Jackson, coming in the back door, said, "Here." He took the strainer to the sink, ran water over it, and handed it to his mother without explanation.

Martha raised an eyebrow, giving it a suspicious frown, and rinsed it again for good measure.

"Give me a hand with this here tea," she commanded the boy.

Jackson held the strainer over the wide-mouthed gallon jar while Mama poured, gripping the full pan carefully with both hands. Steam rose, not scalding hot—just warm and moist enough to mist the window over the kitchen sink.

Martha's eyes evaluated Nathan with a sideways glance. "Change your shirt," she called to the child. "You're soppin' wet."

Nathan looked down at his shirt front, soaked from the dripping ice cube. He patted his chest with a nice, wet, smacking sound, and scampered out of the room.

Martha set the tea on the counter, out of the way, and hesitated. Supper was almost ready, and she was wearied with the effort—more so because her mind was worried. All the children were in, now, and hungry for their dinner. But Lester was still not home. She could never be sure when to expect him. Each day the peach farm laborers stayed until all the work allotted for that day was done. It could be another hour or two before he came home. This was not unusual. And, without a phone in the house, he had no way to get word to her. She didn't like to serve supper to the family without waiting for their father. But sometimes she had no choice.

Whenever Les did come in, he would likely have a paper sack with culls from the day's work—peaches that were misshapen or bruised, or for whatever reason deemed unworthy to pack under the Johnson label. Martha made good use of these, baking them into pies, or cutting them into small slices to soak in milk with a little sugar; she would mash a few very soft ones to give more substance and flavor to the milk. This mixture was then put into bowls and served for dessert. A poor man's peaches and cream. Each bowl had mostly liquid—but everyone got at least a few scraps of peach, along with the sweetly flavored milk.

Martha was a slender woman, serious and plain. She wore her dresses long, sometimes one over another for warmth in winter. A thin, ivory-colored cardigan was her only sweater, and she wore it every day, except in the full heat of summer. Only on Sundays, with her hair neatly brushed and pinned, and wearing her navy blue dress with the white collar, did she resemble the pretty young girl she had once been. Once in a while she wore her own grandmother's white straw hat, the one with pretty, artificial pink roses attached all around the band. Then her cheeks were pink, too.

Today her face was colorless—as pale as her daughter's sand-colored dress. She folded her arms and eyed Maggie from head to toe. "What you been doin' to get mud all over you?" she demanded. Without waiting for an answer, she pointed to the stairs. "Go wash."

Her eyes followed the little girl's every step, until Maggie turned the landing and could be seen no more.

Jackson made a move to go, but his mother's voice arrested him.

"Jackson—"

"Ma'am?"

She pointed to a chair at the kitchen table. "You sit down, right there. I want to talk to you."

Jackson obeyed, watching, apprehensively, while his mother opened the oven door to check once more on the cooling cornbread. She straightened and turned the flame way down under the beans on the stove top.

"What is it, Mama?" he wanted to know. "What's the matter?"

Martha sat down across the table from him. Again a slight frown wrinkled her forehead. She drew a report card from her apron pocket and laid it, portentously, on the table.

"I thought I did okay," Jackson said, returning her frown. "I got mostly A's. 'Cept for English."

"Jackson, this is not your report card," Martha replied with strained patience. "It's your sister's."

She pushed the card across the table so Jackson could read it.

The boy picked it up, reluctantly. He scanned the grades and cast a furtive glance at his mother's face.

Martha pointed to the back of the card. "There's a note."

He turned the card over and silently read in Mrs. Sanders' precise handwriting:

> *Without doubt, Margaret is capable of a far better academic performance than is here indicated—if she would merely expend the required effort. Margaret is consistently inattentive and, not infrequently, uncooperative.*

Jackson laid the card down on the table. He avoided his mother's penetrating gaze.

Martha said, "I want to know what that means, exactly. You understand that kind of school-teacher talk better than I do. You know good and well I never got higher than fifth grade, 'cause my mama needed me at home. So, explain it to me."

She waited.

Slowly Jackson replied, "Maggie never has done too good in school, Mama. That's nothing new."

"That *note* part there is something new." Mama tapped her finger on the handwriting. "I want to know what it means, Jackson. And I aim to find out."

Upstairs, Maggie and Iris were lounging in their shared bedroom, killing time until Daddy got home and they could have their supper. It was getting late and Iris watched at the open window, daydreaming, pondering the wonders of young love. Since the Valentine' Day dance at school, she'd been "going with" Albert Beeson, a senior with his own car. Her life had not been the same. She hummed softly, thinking of his deep brown eyes and wavy hair. He had a man's face. He had to shave every day, and even then by night there was dark stubble along his chin line and upper lip. The thought of his lips made her long to taste them again. She sighed and turned away from the window.

Maggie was playing dominoes in the floor. She didn't stand them up in a line, like most children do, to watch them fall one atop the other. Maggie arranged them in a neat, tightly packed rectangle, two layers deep. Then she lay flat on the floor and observed the way the light from the window affected the edges. She turned her head to observe with her peripheral vision. Then she looked out of the opposite corner of her visual range.

Iris watched her for a moment. "Mags, what *are* you doing?" It was basically a rhetorical question.

Maggie was absorbed. If she heard, she didn't reply.

"Maggie Burnett, I'm talking to you."

Nothing. Not even a glance. Iris rolled her eyes. "You are so majorly weird," she whispered under her breath.

She checked herself in the mirror on the dresser. She was dressed for work. She had been hired as a clerk at the Drug Store in Inman when she turned sixteen. This had opened a whole new world to her. She was allowed to spend a small part of the money she earned on herself—although the bulk had to be given to her mama to help with household expenses. Still, Iris managed an occasional new skirt, cheap jewelry, and hair products. Even more importantly, a real job complete with a name tag meant she was a woman now. Her reflection in the mirror smiled at her. She was pretty, Iris complimented herself with pleasure. Maybe even beautiful. Her skin was clear and every part of her face was in perfect proportion. She decided she was either very, very pretty or slightly beautiful. Having established that, she turned to check on Maggie again.

Now Maggie had lined up all the dominoes, end to end, in one long line to see if they would reach across the bedroom floor.

"Oh, for heaven's sake," Iris said aloud. "Maggie, let me show you how to play a real game with those things, okay? It's not hard."

She made a move to scoop the little blocks into a pile which would make up the "bone yard." But at her first touch, Maggie emitted a sound like an injured animal and crouched protectively over the dominoes.

Iris was mildly stunned. She sat down on her bed. "I was only gonna—"

Maggie made no reply, only continued to hold both hands hovering over the dominoes, as if to shield them.

"What*ever,*" Iris shrugged. "I got to go to work, anyhow. Albert will be here any minute."

She paused, to let Maggie speak, but the child was silent, studying a new pattern to make with the small black rectangles.

Iris felt a little tender hurt in her newly-awakened heart. Her baby sister was sometimes annoying, but Iris cared about her. And worried about her.

"Bye, Mags," she said softly, kissing the girl on top of her head.

"I want a hug," Maggie reminded her.

"Oh, yeah." Iris embraced her while Maggie counted out loud to seven. Then the hug was over. It was a ritual they had fallen into. It helped Maggie through a potentially grievous goodbye.

"Okay, kid," Iris whispered, and was gone.

Downstairs, Martha and Jackson had come to an impasse over the report card, when they were interrupted by the sound of quick footsteps on the stairs.

Iris fluttered into the room, attractively dressed for work in a short-sleeved pink sweater and a grey-pleated skirt. Her skin was scented with Evening in Paris cologne. Her eyes briefly took in the empty table.

"I'll have to get a foot-long at Jody's on the way," she announced. "Mama, can I have fifty cents?"

"You've got fifty cents of your own, child," Martha assured her. "Stay a minute, I want to ask you about something."

"Mama, I can't—I'll be late!"

"Look this over and tell me what you make of it." She pressed the report into her daughter's hand, calmly ignoring the girl's protest.

Iris rolled her eyes. Aloud, hastily, she read, "D, F, C, C-minus, F, unsatisfactory, unsatisfactory—unsatis—"

The girl crinkled her nose, making a face. "You didn't do so good, Mama," she quipped.

"This is not funny, Iris Burnett. Read the back."

Iris flipped the card over, scanned the note and tossed the card onto the table. Her smile had faded.

"Mama, you *don't* want to know," she assured her.

"Oh, yes, I do, and you are not leaving this house until you answer me."

Outside, in the front yard, Albert sat waiting in his 1951 Chevy, the motor idling.

"You want to make me late for work?" Iris attempted the hissy-fit tone she had heard from the other girls at school. It was not very convincing.

"I'm not particularly concerned about whether or not you are late for work, young lady. Explain that note, please."

Iris sighed. She couldn't think of anything but the truth, not with that Chevy purring just outside. "Mama. Mrs. Sanders is saying she thinks Maggie can do better schoolwork than what she's doing."

"It says more than that. Don't mess with me, girl."

The Chevrolet's horn blew impatiently.

"Straight up, Mama—? It says Maggie's not doing good because she's not trying."

Jackson dropped his head onto his crossed arms with a muffled groan. "Way to go, Iris," he mumbled under his breath.

"Well, that's what it says. Can I go now, please? My ride is here."

Martha's face had blanched. "Yes, go. Tell Albert to drive careful."

Iris gave her mother a peck on the cheek and breezed out the door without a backward glance. There was the sound of a car door opening and shutting and then the Chevy roared out onto the dirt road, tires spitting gravel from the small intermittent patches where Lester had tried to make a driveway years ago.

Martha stared, unseeing for a moment.

"Maggie is not trying?" she repeated slowly grasping the seriousness of the situation.

Jackson looked warily at his mother. Her face, formerly perplexed, was now set in firm lines of disapproval.

"Mama," he said carefully, "that teacher, that Mrs. Sanders, she is one mean teacher. I had her myself in fourth grade. She's no good with kids like Maggie. You know—shy kids that scare easy. Special kids. She don't understand 'em, and she don't like them."

He hesitated. He couldn't tell if his mother was listening or not. Her face was like a mask. With effort, he continued. "I don't know why Maggie does poor in school. She's not stupid—"

"That's what I know."

"—and she studies. You know she does, you've seen her doing the best she can with her schoolwork every night. But her mind somehow don't stick well to schoolish things. And that Mrs. Sanders, she's no help, the way she—"

"Don't be tryin' to put blame on the teacher, Jackson."

"I only meant—"

"I know what you meant," Martha said calmly. "I know, also, that being so awful shy is a hardship on Maggie. But she—"

"It's not just shy, Mama," Jackson interrupted. "It's something—more. Deeper. I don't know what. I've tried and tried to figure her out. She's not slow—well, maybe a little. But she's just—different—from the other kids."

That brought up a question of another nature. Martha struggled to bring herself to ask it.

"Do they—Jackson, do they—do the other children make fun of her?" Martha whispered. She had to force herself to speak this painful concern.

"No. Not so much," Jackson consoled his mother. " 'Cause she's just quiet and sweet and doesn't bother anybody. Also she's pretty. And if she has anything, she'll share it. The kids seem to like her; and they all feel sorry for the way the teacher treats her. That Mrs. Sanders —" he shook his head, blowing air out his cheeks. "You'd think it was against the law to be any little bit different. Mama, Maggie don't talk back. I'm tellin' you the gospel truth. She never does anything that's honestly wrong. I'd know. She'd tell me herself, for crying out loud, she's so—so—innocent. Worst thing she does is daydream. A lot. And she keeps a messy desk. That's it."

Martha's brow was furrowed.

"This here is a word I do know. Uncooperative. That's the same as saying she doesn't do what she's told—isn't it?" she queried.

"Does Maggie always mind what you tell her?" Jackson asked pointedly.

Martha thought a moment. Slowly she answered. "Well, yes—mostly. She obeys pretty well, although she dawdles. Or if something catches her attention and distracts her before she—"

"You see?" he pressed. "That's not the same as being uncooperative. Does she ever talk back or be ugly to you?"

Martha shook her head, sadly now.

"Does she ever complain or say 'I don't want to,' like occasionally me or Iris do?—and, Nathan does it all the time and gets away with it, too, 'cause he's the baby."

Martha couldn't resist a small, pitiful smile at that. "Well, honey, a mother gets tired. Sometimes, specially if there's six, she lets the last one get away—yes, it's true—with a little more." She was fully smiling now, because of Jackson's wide-eyed astonishment at her confession. "Parents are just people, too, Jackson. And—we do get tired."

"I'm sorry, Mama," he said gently, chastened. "I'll try to do better. I'll try to help you more with the little ones."

"You're fine, Jackson. You're a good boy," his mother reassured him, getting up from the table. She slid the guilty report card between the salt and pepper shakers.

"But Mama—"

"A note from the teacher can't be ignored, son. Your Daddy will have to know about this. Can't be helped."

Those were the last words Jackson wanted to hear. He leaned back in his chair with a thoroughly frustrated sigh.

Martha stood, ignoring him,. She armed herself with a potholder, and opened the creaking hot oven door. She slid the cornbread out and set it on top of the stove, warm and golden brown.

Young Nathan came prancing through the kitchen, pretending to be a circus pony. His straight blonde hair, long over the eyes, bounced with each step like the mane of a Palamino. Nathan had intended to trot through the kitchen and out again, but the warm, good scent of the cornbread stopped him short.

"I'm hungry," he announced belligerently.

"I'll be calling you to supper soon," his mother said, slicing tomatoes.

Nathan's mouth turned down. "I can't wait," he whined. "I'm hungry now!"

"You better hush that foolishness," Martha said mildly, pointing a meaningful finger toward the backdoor. Martha kept a switch behind the kitchen door, and she was handy with it.

Nathan hushed and walked over to the kitchen table with a frown. He pressed close to Jackson, leaning on his elbows, morosely watching the supper preparations.

Mama poured a small handful of uncooked oatmeal into a little bowl. "This here is what real ponies eat," she said, handing it to Nathan. "You can munch on that while you wait for people food."

Nathan tasted it, made a face, but then ate it all, using his tongue to lick it up from the bowl.

Abruptly his eye fell on Maggie's report card, stuck in between the salt and pepper shakers. With a long stretch across the table he managed to reach it. He took it in both hands, examining the neatly printed words and boxes with curiosity.

Nathan was not yet in school, and though he had heard a great deal about report cards, he had never actually seen one before.

"Can I have this?" he asked his brother.

"Don't be stupid," Jackson mumbled.

"I want it," Nathan persisted. "I want to color on it, with my crowns."

"The word is 'crayons.' And no, you can't." Jackson took the card away from him and placed it back in the middle of the table.

"Mama—" Nathan started.

"You-all hush," she said, without looking around.

Nathan scowled. "I can do what I want with it," he informed his big brother, in a lowered voice. "It's mine—because I found it."

"You didn't find it, you just grabbed it. You start taking things that don't belong to you, and you'll—" Jackson glanced at his mother's back and dropped his voice to a whisper "—you'll end up like your brother Reuben."

Nathan narrowed his eyes. He looked up and saw his mother busy at the stove, her back turned. He twisted his face into the ugliest expression he could conjure up and stuck out his tongue at Jackson.

"Aw, for crying out loud—don't be such a baby," Jackson grumbled, fed up. He bolted out of his chair and disappeared angrily up the stairs.

Nathan looked to his mother. Her back was still turned.

The little boy eyed the report card for a long minute, weighing his brother's words. Then, with sudden determination, he snatched it out from between the salt and pepper shakers.

He became a pony again and galloped out of the room with a whinny, clutching his prize.

Maggie met Jackson at the door of the bedroom she and Iris shared.

"Look," she said eagerly. She held out her hands, cupped loosely together. "I found a bug. It sings."

Jackson steered her into the bedroom and shut the door behind them.

"What's the matter with you?" he demanded in a stern whisper. "Ain't you got sense enough to know when you're in trouble?"

Her face fell. She sat on the edge of the bed, still holding her cricket gently in the warm cavern of her hands.

"Did you *look* at that report card of yours before you handed it over to Mama?" Jackson demanded.

Maggie wasn't sure what answer would be in her best interest at this point. She kept her silence.

"Well, did you?"

"Yes?" she murmured cautiously.

Jackson stared. "Yes? That's all you got to say? Yes?"

Maggie lowered her head. "I didn't do good. I know."

"Didn't—didn't do good??—You did awful!" he informed her, his hands gesturing in frustration. "You understand that? *Awful*!"

Maggie looked at him without expression. The cricket wriggled inside her palms and she lifted her hands and peeked through her fingers to see if it was all right.

"Jackson, will you fix me a little cage or something to keep my cricket in?" she asked.

"No. Absolutely not," he said firmly. "Will you forget about that stupid bug? We got bigger problems."

The cricket, with a sudden bold leap, escaped from between the little girl's fingers and landed on the bed. The jolt of it startled Maggie, and she squealed and clapped her hands to her mouth.

As for Jackson, he was nothing less than stunned by the sheer size and impressive appearance of the cricket. Everything else that had been on his mind was, for the moment, forgotten.

He bent closer to look at it, and gave a long, low whistle of genuine admiration. "I swear, if that ain't the biggest, ugliest cricket I ever laid eyes on," he breathed. "Look at all those spike-looking things on its legs. Man, that is one fine cricket."

Maggie let the "word" slide. There was a more important issue at hand. "It sings so loud, Jackson. It's pretty."

"Crickets don't sing. They chirp."

"Will you make me something to keep it in?" she asked again.

"Nathan used to have a cricket cage, made out of real brass," Jackson recalled. Maggie's eyes widened.

"Daddy won for him at the Fairgrounds, last October. Won it playing the Colors. You remember? Daddy put his quarter down on brown and the ball rolled all around forever on the hole inside of a pink square—and then all of a sudden it just toppled over onto the brown square and dropped right in the hole, like it done it on purpose—like magic or something. You remember that?"

"A real cricket box?" Maggie asked hopefully. "Special for crickets?"

"Yeah. Made in India and carved all pretty with designs and little openings for air. Bright, shiny brass. Just big enough to hold in one hand. Even had a little wooden handle on the lid. And a tiny latch."

Jackson pressed his lips together in a thoughtful frown. "But now that I think on it—I never did see it no more after that night. Nate probably broke it. Or Mama might of throwed it out. On account of winning anything at Colors is gambling, to her way of thinking."

"Anyhow," Maggie said soberly. "I don't want Nathan to know about my cricket."

"You can't hardly keep a thing like a cricket hid," Jackson reasoned. "Not with the racket they make."

"It's singing."

"Chirping, Maggie." He scratched his head with a frown. "But you're probably right about Nathan. He'd likely want it for fish bait."

They had no time to solve the dilemma.

Without warning, the cricket sprang from the bed in a wild bound and landed somewhere in the mass of clutter on top of Iris's dresser.

"Get him!" Maggie cried, leaping up. "Don't let him get away!"

But Jackson had a sudden, happy vision of his older sister reaching into her scattered pile of cheap jewelry for an earring and pulling out the spikey black bug, instead. He leaned back languidly against the headboard of the bed, smiling to himself.

"That cricket's all right," he told Maggie. "He can't hurt himself over there on Iris's dresser. Let him be, awhile. Let him stretch his legs. Least 'til we figure out someplace to keep him."

From outside the open window came the sound of an old-model Buick laboring up the road and into the yard.

Jackson's grin vanished. He bolted upright. Downstairs, the screen door of the porch creaked open and slammed shut.

"There's Daddy home," the boy said, catching his sister's hand and drawing her back to the bed. "Listen to me, and listen good. You're gonna be in serious trouble when Daddy finds out what your teacher wrote on your report card."

Maggie's eyes opened wide. "What. What'd she write?"

"What'd she—didn't you read it?" he exclaimed. "You didn't even read it??"

The girl shook her head, worried now.

"Maggie. You got to listen to me. This is important." He looked into his sister's face, speaking slowly and distinctly. "Mrs. Sanders wrote on your report card that the reason your grades are so bad is because you don't try."

He waited for the full impact of these words to hit her. But she only looked demurely, and a little sadly, down at her hands folded in her lap.

Jackson ran his hands through his hair in exasperation. "Don't you get it, Maggie? When a teacher says you're not trying, that's—that's worse than an F! That's the worst thing a teacher can put on a report card. The absolute *worst*!"

Tears welled up in Maggie's eyes. "I'm sorry," she murmured.

Jackson grimaced. "No, Maggie," he explained, carefully modulating his tone of voice. He wanted to communicate with her, not terrify her. "No. You don't have to be sorry to me. I'm not the one who's mad at you. I want to help you."

Maggie slid closer to him on the bed, laid her head against his bony shoulder, and began to cry softly.

Jackson was so sorry for her, he could hardly stand it. It wasn't fair what Mrs. Sanders had written. It wasn't even true. But Daddy would believe without question whatever a teacher said. Maggie was sure to get a whipping.

From the foot of the stairs their mother's voice called, "You young'uns come on down. Daddy's home and supper's ready."

Jackson took Maggie by both shoulders and sat her up straight. With the frayed cuff of his shirt sleeve, he awkwardly tried to wipe her face dry of tears.

"Listen to me," he said quietly, "You been doin' your schoolwork and all, ain't you?"

She nodded.

"You turned in all your homework?"

Maggie looked uncertain.

Jackson sighed. "Okay. When Daddy asks you about your report card, you got to tell him you *have* been trying. That you done your best. I'll back you up."

From the foot of the stairs came Martha's voice, stronger. "Children? Supper!"

Maggie turned her tearful eyes toward Iris's dresser top. "I can't go down until I find my cricket."

"That cricket's all right," Jackson said, with forced patience. "Pay attention here, Maggie. What did I tell you to say about school?"

"That I tried," Maggie said in a small voice.

"Tried what? Tried your best," he coached her.

She nodded. "—my best."

Jackson rewarded her with a smile. "Good girl. Don't forget, now, okay?"

She nodded again.

"Come on. We got to go down, they're waiting supper on us."

The girl glanced toward the dresser. "I'm not going until I find my—"

Jackson caught her hand and pulled her hurriedly into the hallway.

The kitchen was still warm from the oven and fragrant with comfortingly familiar country fare.

Martha stood pouring milk, while Lester, already seated at the head of the table, talked to her about his day's work. He was absorbed in what he was saying and did not give Maggie and Jackson even a glance as they slipped unobtrusively into their places.

Jackson's eyes immediately flew to the salt and pepper shakers in the middle of the table.

The report card was gone.

The boy frowned, considering various possible explanations, until he saw the card, brightly scribbled with color and somewhat mangled, clutched in Nathan's lap. "What on Earth—? he whispered.

Nathan grinned up at him impishly.

Mama placed a last bowl of steaming vegetables on the table and sat down.

Lester shot a glance around the table at each of his children, to satisfy himself that they were quiet and settled.

"Bow your head, boy," he reminded Nathan. He bowed his own head, then, and mumbled hastily, "Bless this food to our use and us to Thy service, amen."

Jackson opened his eyes and looked at his mother. Maybe with the card out of sight she would forget. She seemed very much interested in hearing about Lester's hard day at work. Besides, she would not bring such a thing up at table and let it ruin her carefully prepared meal.

Jackson stole a glance at Maggie. She was meditatively crumbling the cornbread on her plate into tiny pieces. Cricket-sized pieces, he guessed, shaking his head.

"If we get rain tonight, we'll have to start all over and spray again tomorrow," Lester was saying. He leaned hungrily over his plate, shoveled a huge spoonful of beans into his mouth, and followed it with a chunk of cornbread.

Martha laid down her fork and sat with worried eyes fixed on her husband's lean face. "So are they calling for rain, Les?"

He shrugged, chewing a piece of the fatback together with another bite of cornbread. "Calling for thirty to forty percent chance, like pretty much every day. Only there hasn't been any. When it does come, it'll likely be a heavy rain. Wash every speck of spray down through the gullies. But I don't look for it tonight."

Martha watched her husband eat like a man half-starved. She would never allow one of the children to choke down their food so quickly. But it was not her place to instruct her husband. She knew well that his single bologna sandwich at lunch had been consumed almost nine hours ago. As much as he sometimes aggravated her, she hated to see him so hungry and tired. There was still love in her heart for her husband of twenty-eight years, despite the fact he had turned out to be a very different man than she had known in her youth. He'd had dreams then, hopes—enthusiasm. All long forgotten. He loved his children, but did not take the same kind of tender interest in them that their mother did. His first concern was to provide adequately for those children, and his wife, too. He put his own needs last, if they were met at all. Knowing this, Martha's heart yearned to ease his burdens and comfort him. No doubt he had been disappointed in her over time, as well. She understood the difference between young love and devotion. He was a good man, devoted to his family. Distracted by her thoughts, she let the fork lie loosely in her hand, unused.

"You eat earlier?" Lester inquired, noticing.

"No," she murmured, brushing at her left eye and resuming her meal.

"You need to eat, woman. You're skinny as a twig."

Martha looked at him with a tiny, sad smile, making no reply.

Nathan glanced around the table. Nobody was talking. He saw his chance for a share in the attention, and held up his crayoned artwork to be admired.

But Jackson, sitting beside him, saw it first. He grabbed his little brother's wrist and jerked his arm down.

Nathan turned on him with his chin jutted out, rage in his eyes. There was a brief, almost soundless struggle.

"Hey! What's the matter there," Lester demanded with a frown.

Both boys were instantly still.

Lester squinted his eyes across the table. "What you two fightin' over?"

"Nothin' Daddy," Jackson said, his eyes on his plate.

Lester's frown remained. He was going to say more, but his attention was diverted at that moment by the rumbling of an eighteen-wheeler, growing louder as it reached the dirt road in front of the house.

The truck pulled into the yard, accompanied by the hiss of air brakes and the repeated bellow of a tractor-trailer horn blowing, loud and dissonant.

"Sonny's home!" Nathan cried, leaping from his chair. The report card dropped to the floor, forgotten.

Deftly, Jackson snatched up the card and slid it inside his shirt. He glanced around the table. No one had noticed. All eyes were on the front door as the eldest Burnett boy burst in, catching Nathan in mid-air, and swinging him to his shoulder.

Sonny sauntered into the kitchen with an irrepressible grin.

"Just for the record," he said importantly, "I want you all to know that from here to St. Louie and back is one dadgum miserable long haul. I ain't had the chance even to take a decent shower in going on two weeks."

Lester turned sideways in his chair to greet his firstborn.

"Didn't know what day to expect you, son, but I knew for sure well what time of day—mealtime!" he grinned a little, pointing to an empty chair at the table. "Sit yourself down. Martha, fix the boy a plate."

"Hold off, Mama," Sonny said. "I got to wash up before I can mix with folks, and that's a fact. Just give me ten minutes and don't let these here ragamuffin young'uns eat it all, meantime."

He swung Nate to the floor, leaned to kiss his mother's cheek, and raised a hand hello to Maggie and Jackson. "Iris working?" he asked.

"Every night this week," Martha sighed resignedly. "And they keep her so late."

Sonny nodded indifferently. "Oh, by the way—there was a registered letter for you at the post office, Daddy. Almost forgot." He pulled it from his vest pocket and tossed it on the table. "There you go. Looks important."

Lester picked up the letter quizzically. "Registered—?"

Sonny started for the stairs. He said to Jackson, "Whatsa matter with you? You can't say hello to somebody?"

Sonny gave the boy a friendly cuff that knocked him halfway out of his chair, and bounded up the stairs without waiting for an answer.

Lester studied the opened letter with a frown of concentration.

"Bad news, Les?" Martha asked quietly, worried.

The sound of her voice startled him. He looked up and saw the eyes of his children fastened anxiously on his face.

"No—nothing bad," he mumbled vaguely. He frowned at the letter again. Then he met his wife's questioning gaze. "It's from my Aunt Irene, in Kentucky," he explained. "You remember her, don't you? Little spinster woman—not much to look at?"

Mama frowned. "That's unkind, Lester. And yes, I remember her."

"Listen to this here," Lester said. "She's met some fellow from Texas, up to visit his kinfolk in the Bluegrass—they been courting, and have decided to get married."

"Well, whoever would have thought!" Martha declared, wiping tomato seeds from Nathan's cheek with her napkin.

Lester nodded soberly. "She sounds right tickled about it. He's a widow-man, lonesome since his wife died. She's all in a dither, packing—making ready to move to Houston."

"Houston, Texas?" Martha exclaimed.

"That's where this widow-man is from. I said that once already, if you'd a been listening."

Martha looked thoughtful. She pointed to the letter. "That's not an invitation to the wedding, I hope? She's not expecting a gift from us?"

Lester rubbed his hand over his chin in a distracted sort of way. "Not a gift, exactly."

"She wants something, though," Martha surmised, grimly.

Lester drew a deep breath. "My grandmother—on my father's side—she's been living all this time with my Aunt Irene," he explained.

"Your grandma—the one folks call Miss Mae?" Martha said. "I remember her, Les. Mercy, I would of thought she'd passed on by now."

"Eighty-nine year old," Lester said, raising the letter slightly in answer. "She won't be moving with Irene to Texas. But then, she ain't able to stay by herself no more, either." Lester hesitated. "Long years back, Miss Mae lived right here in this house—did you know that?"

Martha's eyes widened. "This house? *Our* house?"

He nodded again, his eyes fixed on the letter. His voice was low. "It was her house, then. She grew up here, when it was still a kept-up place. She gave the house over to my father, free and clear, when she moved to Kentucky to live with Irene."

"I never knew that," Martha declared.

Lester cleared his throat softly. "According to this letter—according to Irene—my grandma wants to come home, now."

Martha stared. "Home—?" she asked, stunned. "You don't mean here?"

He gave a single, stoic nod.

"Lester Burnett, are you trying to tell me your grandmother that we've hardly even met is askin' to come here to *our* house and *live* with us?"

Lester folded the letter and put it back inside the envelope. He drew a troubled sigh. "It was her house before it was ever ours. She's got no place to go, now—if we don't take her in."

"Sounds to me like your mind's made up already," Martha said tersely.

Lester nodded. "It is."

Lester sat on the front porch that night, gazing morosely at the clear black sky glittered with stars. Nights like this, he wished fervently to have back one of his old vices—cigarettes. Something to do with his restless hands and thoughts.

He only half-turned his head when the screen door creaked open, not actually looking. Not needing to. He knew each of his children by the weight of their footsteps on the worn wooden floor.

"Take a load off," he invited his oldest son, pointing to the chair beside him.

Sonny sat down with a satisfied sigh. "Don't mind if I do," he said congenially. He liked being on the road, but he liked being home, too. The constant shift between the two, the rhythm of his young adult life, seemed to him the best of all possible worlds. In his middle teens he'd worked alongside his friends, hauling baskets of peaches to the big trucks. He'd known then what he planned to do when he got his driver's license and whatever other license would be required. When he made his first run, he knew he had found his calling. Not once did he miss working with peaches. Neither did he miss his family or friends. He was made for life on the move.

Although he didn't miss the family, he did think of them. It was great to come home now and again and be hailed like some kind of hero because he had a good-paying, respectable job.

For several minutes neither man spoke, both lost in their respective thoughts and mutually content to listen to the crickets and the frogs and the occasional cicada make their incredibly strange and beautiful night songs.

"What's your Mama doin'?" Lester inquired after a time.

"Getting Nate to bed."

Lester frowned. "Late for that."

"He'd been asleep once, and woke up. Had a bad dream, I'm guessin' from all his squallin' and carrying on."

His daddy snorted. "What's a young'un his age got to dream about?"

Sonny grinned. "Snakes, it sounded like—what I could make out. I don't dream, myself. Never did. They say ever'body dreams, but it ain't so."

It was Lester's turn to smile. "You needn't sound so fat and sassy. You used to talk in your sleep. I expect you was dreaming."

"When did I talk in my sleep," Sonny challenged. "What'd I say?"

Lester looked back out at the sprinkle of stars in the night sky. He only smiled, without answering.

Sonny shrugged. His conscience was reasonably clear. Clear enough to suit him, anyway. He tipped his chair up on its back legs, leaning it against the wall of the house, and laid his right ankle comfortably across his left knee.

Lester didn't look at him, but felt his presence with satisfaction. He was well-pleased with his first-born son. The offspring of his own youth.

Life had not been so hard in those days. He and Martha had been married less than a year, still caught up in the glow of first love, when Sonny was born. Never had he felt the power of his manhood as he did then. Never had he been so proud as when he carried that infant boy in the crook of his arm.

But the babies had kept coming. Another boy, and then a girl. His pretty young bride began to be a pale, exhausted mother. Little Iris was not yet in school when Jackson came along. Three years after that, Maggie. And finally Nate. At least, he sure hoped Nate would be the final one. Not that he didn't love his children. He did. But any more would be a crippling burden on their lean finances, as well as an emotional and physical hardship on Martha.

Lester drew a deep sigh. The years had turned his delicate young sweetheart bride into a strong-minded and hard-working woman. Still, he loved her. And was determined that he always would. But he grieved because the laughter had all but gone out of their love.

He did not realize that the years had changed him, too. His once good-natured face was lined from much frowning, from worry, hardened like leather by the sun. He did not know that he had stored a heavy weight of silent anger in his heart—anger at nothing, at everything—at life, for being different than he had envisioned it.

Lester looked down at his hands in his lap and wished again for a cigarette. He folded his arms and cleared his throat.

"I'm glad to see the stars—clear sky and no clouds," he told his son. "We sprayed the whole orchard today."

Sonny didn't need to be told what a task that was. Neither was he ignorant of the repetition required if rain came too soon. He nodded his understanding.

"Son," Lester began delicately, "you said you was planning to give up smoking. Did you do it?"

"I sure did, Daddy."

"Aw, that's great. That's a good thing. You made a good decision on that one, boy."

There was a pause.

For the sake of complete honesty, Sonny amended, "Well...mostly."

"Mostly?" Lester perked up. He even sat up straighter. "Mostly, you say? So sometimes you still—?"

"Yeah, sometimes. But hardly ever. Don't worry. I won't let the kids see me smoking."

"I appreciate that." Lester nodded. He turned his eyes out into the night with a heavy sigh, unaware that he was still nodding.

"Daddy?"

"Hm?"

Sonny suppressed an amused chuckle. "Daddy, do you want a cigarette?" he offered, pulling a half-full pack from a hidden inner pocket in his jacket.

Lester's tight shoulders relaxed like melted ice cream. "Sonny, my boy, of all my six children—you're the keeper."

Sonny laughed out loud at that. He extended his dad a smoke and lighted it with a quick strike of a match. Lester received it almost with reverence.

After one long draw, he smiled as nothing had made him smile in a long time.

"No need for your mother—"

"—no need at all," Sonny agreed.

The two men smoked together in one accord, saturated in contentment. Long moments passed in easy silence.

Then Lester's brow furrowed. "Your Mama's not keen on Grandma Burnett coming," he said.

Sonny was unconcerned. "She'll manage. You know Mama."

"It ain't right, though, putting that kind of burden on Martha," Lester murmured, thinking out loud. "But it wouldn't be right, neither, to turn my grandma away, after she give this house to my father. And then outlived him." Lester shook his head. "I wouldn't rest easy if I didn't do right by her, best I can."

"Yes, sir, I can understand that all right." Sonny dropped his chair back down level and uncrossed his legs. He leaned forward thoughtfully for a moment.

"I don't know how you do it, Daddy," Sonny said with admiration. "I worked in peaches every summer since I was fourteen until I got my trucking license. That's some hard, back-breaking work. You're gettin' a little age on you, y'know."

"*Don't* I know?!" Lester gave a low whistle. "Aw, it's what you get used to. People can do most anything when they have to."

"I reckon that's so."

Sonny fell quiet. His handsome blonde coloring shone like gold in the moonlight. He finished his cigarette, tapped it out, and still did not speak. It didn't take long for his father to notice.

"You got something on your mind, Son?"

"Well—yes, sir," he admitted, then fell silent.

Lester crushed his cigarette under his shoe and threw the stub as far from the house as possible. Martha need not know he had backslidden this once. Unless she gave him a goodnight kiss, he realized belatedly. Oh, well. She wouldn't scold. That was one of the things he valued most in her.

Time passed in slightly awkward silence. Sonny waited for his father to ask, but Lester wouldn't press. This son was a fully grown man. He'd already invited him to speak his mind. Now it was up to him.

The crickets and frogs chorused louder as the night air grew damp and cool. Even a few birds were still singing, right into the dark hours, as if it were still dusk.

Sonny spoke quietly into the chirping orchestration of night noises.

"Daddy," he said slowly, with considerable reluctance. "There's something—something I need to ask you. That is—something I'm supposed to tell you."

Lester frowned. "Something you need to ask? Say what you mean, boy."

"You won't like it."

"I won't like it none the better for having to listen to you beat around the bush," Lester warned him.

But their conversation was interrupted by the arrival of Iris and Albert, his car roaring up the road and spinning into the driveway in the same reckless hurry with which it had left.

"That Iris?" Sonny puzzled. "Awful late, ain't it?"

"Yes—it—is," Lester soberly agreed, his eyes hard on the vehicle stopping in front of his house.

Iris slid out of the car with a little wave goodbye and danced up the porch steps. She stopped in her tracks, surprised to see Sonny.

"When'd you get home?" she said, giving her older brother a peck on the cheek.

"Tonight. Suppertime."

"Of course." Iris grinned.

"Why is everybody picking on me about that?" Sonny wanted to know, feigning innocence.

"I wonder," his sister laughed.

Her father had not spoken. Now he commented, "It's late. The drug store's been closed a couple hours at least. Where you been, girl?"

Iris' smile paled. "Riding around. It's a pretty night. We had the top down. It was real nice with the cool breeze blowing." She gulped, studying her father's face.

"You come straight home next time, hear?"

"Yes, sir, Daddy."

Sonny winked at her and she suppressed a smile.

"Goodnight y'all," she murmured, starting toward the door.

"And don't be givin' your mama anything to worry about. I think you know what I mean."

"Yes, sir," she said quickly and was gone, not pausing an instant for any more questions.

Inside the house, leaning against the closed door, she took a deep breath, eyes closed. As she let it out, she opened her eyes in two wide blue circles. Who would have thought Daddy and Sonny would still be up, sitting on the front porch, going on midnight?

"My lousy luck," she murmured, climbing up the stairs to get ready for bed. She sure hoped Mama was asleep already.

Out on the porch, Lester picked up the thread of conversation. "You had something you were gonna tell me."

Sonny spoke softly. "I heard from Reuben."

Lester's eyes flew to his son's face. The young man returned the gaze, his features dim in the near-darkness, blurred in shadow. His eyes alone, like living things, caught the moonlight.

"Heard from him—?"

"I saw him and talked to him. He was working at a truckstop on 85. Janitor."

Lester gave a short, hard nod. "Go on."

Sonny turned his face away. "He's out, Daddy—he's out on parole."

Lester was painfully silent.

"He was wondering if—you know, if—" Sonny hesitated, stumbling over his words. Lester did not help him. "Thing is, Daddy—he'd like to come back home and stay for awhile. Kind of—get his head together, make some plans, you know. He wanted me to ask you would it be all right?"

For a long moment, Lester just shook his head. When he finally spoke, his voice was pained and introspective.

"I don't know what went wrong with Reuben," he murmured. "I never did. I've given it a lot of thought. From the start, he was just opposite of you. You always were a happy little fella. But Reuben..."

Sonny looked down at his hands self-consciously.

"With Reuben—" his father continued. "We didn't treat him no different. But he just had a kind of moodiness about him—you could see it in his eyes. Like he was—restless. Unsatisfied. Just born that way, seemed like." Lester drew a deep, troubled breath. "Ever once in a while, I think I see a trace of that same look in Nathan."

Sonny shook his head. "Naw, Daddy," he said confidently. "Nathan's right as rain. Nathan's my buddy."

Lester seemed to wake from a light dream. He stirred. His voice became matter-of-fact, void of emotion. "We done what we could for Reuben, your Ma and I did. He's twenty-four year old, now—he's a grown man. He's on his own. It can't be no other way. I got four young'uns still at home to consider. And now my grandmother, too."

Sonny made no reply. There was an uneasy silence.

Lester looked sideways at Sonny. "Don't you say nothing about this to your Mama," he decreed.

Sonny shook his head. "No, sir." He tipped his chair back against the house and folded his arms across his chest, staring soberly out at the black night.

Lester hesitated. "Will you be talking to your brother again?"

"Yes, sir," Sonny said, subdued. "He gave me a phone number. I told him I would call after I talked to you—give him an answer."

Lester spoke haltingly, weighing his words. "Tell him that—I wish—I wish things could of been different. Tell him—well—tell him that I send my regards."

Sonny nodded firmly, without a word, his eyes fixed on the brightly beaded sky.

Lester sighed. "I don't know no more to say, Son."

"It's all right, Daddy."

"We can't have him around here. We just—can't."

"Daddy," Sonny said with unaccustomed gentleness, "it's okay. I understand."

"Well, I know you and him were buddies back in the day."

"Like you say, that was back when."

"I don't know how it might affect the little ones—Maggie and Nathan." Sonny nodded his understanding.

A good ten minutes passed without further conversation. An owl called from its hidden haunt in the woods. The light upstairs turned off. Even the air had changed, becoming cool and whispery.

"My own son asks to come home, and my answer is no," Lester mused in a low voice. "Miserable, hard word. It tastes like metal. Cold and bitter in my mouth. I can't rid myself of the taste of it." He rubbed his forehead and face.

Sonny shook out another cigarette, lighted it and handed it to his father without a word. This time Lester didn't smile. He merely put it to his lips, and smoked wearily.

Part Two

It was a clear and shining sunny day when Mae Burnett returned to her childhood home.

Lester drove alone to the bus station in town to meet her.

Mama dusted everything in sight for the third time in two days, muttering to herself all the while. The children stayed out of her way.

Jackson, at her insistence, had taken Nathan out back to play.

From their upstairs bedroom, Maggie and Iris watched for Daddy's car, restless and bored.

"I can't believe Mama agreed to let that old lady come live with us," Iris mumbled, tossing the window curtain away from her, as she strode back to her bed. "She don't want her. It's plain as day. This here is Mama's house, and she oughtn't to have to let nobody stay here she don't want."

"Daddy says—it was his grandma's house. First," Maggie reminded her.

"Oh, hush," Iris snapped back. "I'm not talking to you."

Maggie's eyes swept the room in a single glance. She wondered who Iris was talking to, if not her.

Iris ignored her. She went to her dresser and rummaged in her purse, searching for gum. All she could find was a piece of pink bubblegum that had been buried in there for an undefined length of time. Iris painstakingly peeled and picked at the stuck paper wrapper until she managed to get most of it off. She popped the gum into her mouth.

"I just know this grandmother business is going to mess up my life," she said thickly. "Worse than the pitiful mess it already *is*, I mean," she clarified, arching her eyebrows. "Mama's gonna want me to babysit that old woman and—and read to her—and fetch things for her." Iris shuddered. "It makes me near out of my mind, just thinking about it."

Maggie had ceased listening to her. She was inspecting the tin band-aid box which was currently serving as home to her pet cricket.

Jackson had punched holes in the box, so the cricket could breathe. Still, it was very small living quarters, Maggie thought, for such a large cricket. Every now and then she opened the box lid a tiny crack to check on her insect friend, taking care not to let him escape. By the time Daddy's car finally rolled into the yard, Maggie had all but forgotten what it was that she and her sister had been so restlessly awaiting.

Iris sprang to the window, determined to get the first look at their great-grandmother.

Maggie, remembering now, was also curious. She stood back a little, craning her neck to be able to see down to the yard below, while remaining hidden from view.

In somber silence they watched their father get out of the car and walk around to the passenger's side.

He opened the door and offered his hand to his grandmother.

Everything after that appeared to the girls to be happening in slow-motion.

Mae Burnett turned slowly in her seat and put one foot out. Then, incredibly slowly, the other foot. Her shoes were heavy and brown, old-fashioned lace-ups. Above them her ankles were unnaturally thick.

Iris, quite unnecessarily, muttered under her breath, "That's her. That's the old lady."

Maggie gave her sister a sideways glance, but Iris didn't notice. Her eyes were fastened on the newcomer. She popped her bubble gum nervously.

When both her feet were settled securely on the ground, Mae reached out a trembling hand, unsteadily, for the support of Lester's arm.

"I am going crazy already," Iris vowed, raising her eyes to the ceiling. "She is making me crazy as a bedbug, and she ain't even in the house yet. If there's one thing I can't stand, its slow old people! Look at this—it's gonna take her forty-five minutes just to get out of the car!"

Maggie saw Lester glance up at the window. She jerked herself hastily out of sight.

"I think he heard you," she whispered, wide-eyed.

Iris dismissed Maggie's worry with a careless wave of her hand. She popped her gum, frowning down on the scene below.

In an instant, she stopped chewing, her mouth agape.

"Now that is what I call some *white* hair," she breathed. She waved her hand dramatically at Maggie. "C'mere. C'mere and look at this. Tell me that's not the snow-whitest hair you ever saw in your life?"

Maggie frowned and turned away from Iris. She wasn't going anywhere near that window. She picked up a necklace from the dresser and held it across her chest, studying the reflection in the mirror.

"They're coming up on the porch now," Iris reported in a loud whisper. "I reckon they'll be all the way to the door in another half hour or so." Iris grinned sarcastically.

Maggie mumbled, "I don't want to know."

Iris let the window curtain fall from her hand. "Can't see 'em no more," she fretted, bored again.

She sat down on her bed with a plop, leaned back against the pillow, and noticed Maggie playing with her jewelry. "Hey, get out of my stuff," she complained.

Maggie put down the necklace and climbed onto her own bed.

Iris leaned her head back and stared morosely at the ceiling. "I hate this. Don't you just hate having some stranger move in with us?" she muttered, not waiting for an answer. "I do. I plain can't stand it. Like it wasn't bad enough already, living out here in the boon-docks, too far to have friends over, and too pitiful to even own a telephone. I swear, sometimes I just plain can't stand it."

From the foot of the stairs their mother's voice called up, "Girls? Iris, Maggie—? Come down here and say hello to your Daddy's grandma."

Iris rolled her eyes. She sank down lower on the bed and grumbled, "My life is over, that's all. Mama's gonna have me tending to that old lady, sure as I'm living and breathing, I know it! She'll probably make me quit my job at the drugstore, and turn me into a full-time old-people babysitter! My life is ruined!"

Iris pulled the bed pillow over her head as if to suffocate herself. She pushed it tightly around her whole face and emitted a scream—barely audible through the spongy foam stuffing.

Then, abruptly, she sat up, threw the pillow aside, and looked around the room.

"Maggie, you seen my fingernail file? I got a ragged nail."

Maggie shook her head.

"Well, you're no help," Iris grumbled, going to her dresser and rummaging through the mess on top. "I got to fix it. I got a date—I mean, I got to work tonight. That is, if Mama don't put me to granny-sitting before then—oh, here it is."

She sat down again on her bed and began vigorously filing the broken nail. Fingernail dust floated down onto her dark skirt like a tiny snowfall. She brushed it off briskly.

"*Girls*—?" came Mama's voice, more distinctly.

Iris rolled her eyes. "You go down, Maggie. Tell her I'm dressing for work."

Maggie shook her head solemnly. "Not me."

"You'll get in trouble if you don't," Iris warned her. "Mama's done called twice."

"She's calling you, too."

"All right," Iris conceded with an unhappy sigh. "We're gonna have to do this sooner or later, I reckon. Come on. We'll go together and get it over with." She held out a hand to Maggie.

Maggie withdrew to a corner of the bedroom and sat down in the floor with her knees pulled up to her chin.

"Come on," Iris urged, flapping her hand at the child.

But Maggie shook her head no.

Iris rolled her eyes in complete exasperation. "Fine. You can do what you please. I'm gone." She swept out the door in a huff, leaving her little sister behind.

Mae Burnett had been given the only downstairs bedroom in the house, the one that had once been Sonny's.

Mama hung fresh white curtains at the windows, and laid down a little clean rag rug beside the bed. It was the sunniest room in the house, which Mama said would be good for Mae because of the amount of time she would probably spend sitting in it. She had even moved the good rocker down from Nathan's room, the one with soft, built-in cushions. This room would be Mae's, now, for as long as she needed it, Mama had stiffly informed the rest of the family.

"I know you must be tired after that long bus ride," Mama said loudly. "Why don't you take a little rest?" Mae made no reply. Mama helped her get settled down for a nap. She came out of the room and drew the door half-closed behind her.

Nathan came racing into the house, with Jackson in hot pursuit. Jackson caught up with the little boy in the kitchen, and slung him upside down across his shoulder.

"Sorry, Mama," Jackson said. "He got away from me."

Mama pointed toward the back door. "Just go," she said wearily. "Both of you."

"Yes'm." Jackson started out and then turned back, still carrying Nate across his shoulder. "Mama, we are gonna be allowed back in the house *sometime*, aren't we?"

She was not amused. "Outside. Now."

Jackson nodded. "If Nate gives me any more trouble, can I take him down in the woods and feed him to the snake?"

Nathan was an instant bundle of hysterical kicking and screaming. "Let me down! Mama—! Make him let me go—!"

Jackson clapped his hand over the little boy's mouth and hurried out the back door, muttering, "I was kidding, for crying out loud. Can't you take a joke?"

Martha stood by the kitchen table with arms folded, watching her husband sip at a mug of hot coffee.

"You and your grandma talk on the way back from town?" she asked pointedly.

"Not much," he said.

"What'd you talk about?" she persisted.

Lester didn't answer.

Martha sat down. "I tried to greet her friendly, Lester. I told her to come on in the house and make herself at home. All she did was smile a little bit, nod. Didn't say two words to me. Didn't say *one* word."

Lester put down his coffee mug and leaned back in his chair with a heavy sigh. For a moment he just studied Martha's questioning face.

"Grandma had a stroke last winter," Lester reluctantly informed his wife. "It affected her speech and slowed her down a little bit. Nothing more."

"A stroke. I see. Irene didn't mention *that* in her letter," Martha said starchily.

"It wouldn't have made no difference."

"I had thought she might help a bit in the kitchen or something, once in a while. Carry her weight a little."

Lester's voice was stubborn. "She belongs to this family, now. What she can do or can't do makes no difference at all."

"No difference to *you*, maybe."

Lester looked hard at his wife. The expression in his eyes was both hurt and angry. "I must say, I thought better of you than that."

"Well, I reckon you thought better of me than you ought," Martha snapped. She stood and left the kitchen without a backward glance.

Lester looked at the clock on the wall. He had no time to argue with his wife just now. He had lost two hours' pay in the time-off he had taken to meet Mae Burnett at the bus station.

He left his coffee unfinished and hurried upstairs to change into his work clothes.

In the upstairs hallway, Lester paused. He tapped on the door to Maggie's room. There was no answer. He pushed the door open.

Maggie, still sitting in the corner with her arms folded around her knees, raised her head.

"Didn't you hear your Mama calling you to come downstairs?" Lester wanted to know.

Maggie lowered her eyes.

Her Daddy's voice hardened. "Answer me."

She murmured, "Yes, sir."

"Why didn't you come down, then?"

She shrugged her shoulders and hid her face in her arms.

Lester studied his youngest daughter with a frown.

"Now you listen here," he said sternly. "That's your great-grandma down there. She's family, you understand? She's here to stay, and you're all gonna have to get used to havin' her around. And I'll tell you something else. I expect every one of you to treat her decent."

Maggie still sat crouched in the corner with her face hidden. She made no response.

Lester felt his temper rise. He took a step forward. "Hey—do you hear me talking to you, girl? Look up here at me!"

Maggie's head jerked up, and her startled eyes flew to his face.

Lester himself was startled. He had wanted her attention, but he had not meant to frighten her. He lowered his voice, taking care to speak calmly. "I want you to go downstairs and say hello to Grandma Mae down there, and make her welcome, all right? That's all I'm asking you to do."

Maggie whispered, "Yes, sir."

Lester gave her a scrutinizing look. "All right, then," he said slowly. "I got to go to work, now. I'll be asking your mama, when I get home tonight, to see if you done what I told you."

Maggie nodded.

"All right, then," Lester said again, in a conciliatory tone.

He hesitated in the doorway, still troubled by a feeling of remorse. This child was not like his others. He forgot sometimes how easily frightened she was.

But he could think of nothing to say to her, at the moment, to smooth things over. And every minute that passed was making him later for work, and being deducted from his pay.

He stepped into the hall without further comment, closing the door behind him.

Maggie sat motionless for some time after her father left, grateful to be alone again. In a little while she picked up the band-aid box and peeped in at her pet cricket.

The cricket rubbed its face delicately with a furry front leg, as if it had been roused from sleep. It's head tilted and seemed to peer back at Maggie in a friendly, curious way.

Cheered by this, Maggie got up from the floor. She put the cricket's box back on her dresser, touching the perforated lid with a kiss from her fingertip.

"Back in a minute," she promised. She tiptoed downstairs on bare feet, as silent as a shadow.

Mae Burnett sat in the rocking chair by her window, gazing out at the wide-spreading branches of the maple tree in the front yard.

She remembered that very tree from when she had lived in this house as a child. It had been scarcely more than a sprig, then, no taller than her mother's shoulder, and no bigger around than her own tiny wrist.

Mae's eyes misted. That was long, very long, ago. Time had changed so many things.

The house itself—she'd had such shining memories of it! But upon arriving, she had found the house old and grey, and sadly in disrepair. It needed paint. The flower beds wanted tending.

Mae Burnett rocked, considering. Most of all, she decided, the house was missing a certain light-heartedness which had once echoed within its walls.

She had not expected to be welcomed with great affection by this grandson she hardly knew, or his family. Yet Lester's grim demeanor had taken her by surprise.

And the wife, Martha—her welcome had been briskly efficient, almost businesslike. There had been no touch on her shoulder, no kiss for her cheek. Not even a smile.

Well, it was that way, sometimes, with adults—feeling, as they did, the weight of responsibility. It would be different with the children, she'd told herself hopefully. Young folks had always taken a liking to her.

But the girl, Iris, would not even look her in the face. She only offered a cold, limp handshake, and mumbled something about having to get ready to go to work. And then Martha, under the guise of letting her rest from the trip, had also gone away—leaving her here, her first afternoon home, all alone.

Mae rocked harder, fighting back a fresh rush of tears. Oh, if only that stroke had not stolen her speech. In the old days she could recite poetry, tell stories, carry on brilliant conversations. She'd had a beautiful alto voice, and had sung in the church choir, right up until the time of her stroke.

Now people seemed to feel uncomfortable in her presence. They avoided her, assuming that she was deaf, or senile, because she could not speak. Her thoughts were clear as a bell, Mae fretted—there was nothing wrong with her mind, only her words. And what were words, after all? People depended on them entirely too much.

She found herself thinking of Irene, and missing her, as she had known she would. She missed, too, their cozy apartment in Kentucky. But it was good that Irene had found a husband with whom to share her retirement years. She was very happy for her daughter, Mae reminded herself stubbornly. Entirely happy.

A lonely chill swept over her body. She was turning to reach for the afghan on her bed, when a slight movement in the doorway caught her eye.

A child hovered half-behind the doorway. She was felt more than seen. Like a wild bird hidden in the forest foliage, Mae thought, like an angel lost. Mae strained her eyes, peering through her thick glasses toward the half-open door.

The shadow all but disappeared.

Her heart sank. She had always been good with children. It used to be so easy. She dared not use her voice now. She could only make animal-like grunts and squeals, not even a simple syllable since the stroke. The pain of this loss washed over her afresh. Nevertheless, she tried again. In total silence, Mae smiled hopefully, motioning with her fingers an invitation to come in.

Maggie came, on soft bare feet. She stood in silence, carefully out of reach of Mae's gently outstretched hand.

The elderly lady waited.

"I'm to say hello," Maggie murmured, without expression. "And—" she hesitated, trying to remember the word Daddy used. "And—um—and—welcome."

She gave a sigh of relief. She could leave now. At least, that was her plan.

Mae gestured for her to come closer. She took a step backward, instead, shaking her head.

Mae's hand drooped quietly to her lap.

Maggie saw, with chagrin, that tears had welled up in her great-grandmother's eyes. Mae's eyes were cloudy blue, and looked very large and gentle and soft behind her thick glasses. The tears looked large, too.

Poor Maggie tried, a little desperately, to think why Mae would be crying. Surely it couldn't be anything she had said. But if Mama came in and saw tears, Maggie would get the blame.

"Don't cry," she implored, filled with sudden dread. "Please don't cry."

Mae shook her head gently.

Maggie cast an anxious glance at the door. "—because if you cry, you'll—you'll get me in trouble."

The elderly lady bowed her head into her hand, trying to control her emotions. Tiny sobs, barely audible, escaped her.

Maggie edged her way, backward, out of the room. Probably the safest thing was simply to be nowhere around, if Mama did come to check on Mae. Stealthily she slipped out the back door. She leaped down the porch steps and took off running in search of her brothers.

Jackson and Nathan were still in the back yard.

Maggie didn't see them at first, because they were up in the big oak tree, half-reclining against its huge, slanting branches.

"Give me a hand up," Maggie begged, when she discovered where they were. "Hurry."

She put one foot against the tree trunk, and Jackson, grabbing her extended hand, swung her easily up to the branch beside him.

"What's up?" he wanted to know.

"Nothing," she said shakily.

"You look like you seen a ghost."

"What you think of —grandma?" Maggie asked her older brother.

"I haven't got to see her yet," he said. "You?"

Maggie shrugged. She wasn't sure if she wanted anyone to know she had been in Mae's room or not.

"What's Nate got?" she asked, seeing that the boy was chewing.

He solemnly opened his damp, purple-stained hand to show her several large early blackberries.

"I want one," she instantly pleaded.

Nathan dutifully picked out one blackberry and dropped it into her outstretched palm.

The taste was delectably sweet, with an underlying tartness. She savored it dreamily. All thoughts of Grandma were gone in an instant. The sweetness aroused the latent hunger crouching in her stomach, causing it to growl. Nathan giggled.

"More," she begged.

"You said one," he protested.

"I don't care. Share, okay?"

Nate shook his head. "You ain't getting no more of mine. You can go hunt 'em yourself."

"Give me just one more? Please?"

Nathan scowled fiercely. "No!"

Maggie lunged for the blackberries, which Nathan snatched away, lost her balance and nearly toppled out of the tree.

Jackson, with lightning quick reflexes, grabbed her arm in time.

He yanked her upright to safety and smacked her bare leg, once, with his open hand.

"You want to break your goosey little neck? Y'all quit fighting," he commanded, frowning. "before somebody gets hurt."

"You made me drop the biggest one!" Nathan declared in a huff.

Sorry, Nate," Maggie said meekly.

The little boy scrambled down the tree, awkwardly, and as he fumbled for a hold, the remaining berries fell from his grasp, hit the hard ground knotted with tree roots and rolled moistly through the loose red dirt. Even Nathan didn't want them now. He took off running toward the house.

"I didn't mean to—" Maggie apologized.

Jackson told her, "Forget it. He can find more in the woods over there. They came in early this year."

Maggie leaned back against the wide oak branch, comfortably, and looked up through the layers of restlessly stirring leaves. The oak tree was one of her favorite places in all the world. She had begged Mama to let her bring a pillow and blanket, and make a bed for herself in the crook of the branches. She had begged to spend the night there.

"When I grow up," Maggie said dreamily, aloud, "I can come up here and sleep in this tree. All night. Nobody can tell me what to do, then."

Jackson yawned. "Yeah, but by then you won't want to sleep in a tree," he informed her. "That's the catch."

Maggie sat partway up, propped on her elbows. "What?" she inquired with a faint frown.

"When you're a grown up, you won't want the same things you want now," he told her patiently. "That's just how it is."

"I will," Maggie declared staunchly. "I will want to." The idea that time could play such a mean trick on her frightened Maggie. She vowed to still want all the same things she wanted now, even when she was grown. The exact same things. And she would have them, too.

"Fine," her brother replied indifferently. He had his pocket knife out, now, and was whittling a scrap of wood.

"You don't believe me," she challenged.

"Nope."

Maggie lay back down, saddened. Her hair was dotted with tiny fragments of tree bark which the wind had blown over her. A large olive-green leaf broke from its moorings and sailed from a high branch downward, rocking back and forth on the air. Maggie watched it, intrigued, to the very moment it landed delicately on her own outspread skirt.

Maggie took the leaf carefully in both hands. She received it with reverence, as a living thing—a wild creature who had consciously chosen to come to her. For a long moment she was silent, cherishing this bit of life so fraught with meaning.

She had forgotten the blackberries, forgotten her brother's disbelief in her, forgotten even having run away from Mae's crying.

But the high-pitched sound of Nathan's voice beneath her was a startling reminder. "Maggie!—Mama wants you."

She sat up, instantly alert.

At the foot of the tree stood Nathan, his face turned upward, watching to see if she'd heard him.

"Why? What for?" she demanded guiltily.

Nathan shrugged. "She just told me to fetch you." He turned with utter indifference and walked back toward the house.

Maggie looked to her older brother. He had been whittling all the while she daydreamed, and had nearly completed a clean little oak whistle. He put it to his lips and blew. The sound was faint and unmelodic, a mere rushing of air. Jackson frowned.

"Jackson," she said in a sudden burst of confession. "I think I made the old lady cry."

His eyes flew to her face. "You *what?*" he demanded in disbelief. "What did you do to her?"

"I don't know. I—I said—hello. And she put out her hand, like this—" Maggie demonstrated. "But I didn't touch it. And then she started crying."

"You should've taken her hand," Jackson said somberly.

"I didn't want to."

"Did I say anything about want-to? You should of anyway," he insisted.

83

"Would you?"

"No," he admitted, begrudgingly. "What else did you say?"

"I don't know. I don't remember. I—I think I told her not to cry?" Maggie wrinkled her nose, shrugging, anxious lest her brother tell her this was a terrible thing to have done.

Jackson merely rolled his eyes.

"Well, what was I supposed to do?"

"I don't know, Magsie. Is that what Mama wants you for?"

"I don't know. If she found out, it is. And if she did find out, and she tells Daddy—I'm in big trouble."

"You got that right."

Jackson folded his knife and slid it in his pocket, along with the whistle. He stood up carefully on the wide branch and poised himself to jump down.

"What am I gonna do?" Maggie pleaded.

"Hang on," he told her. He sprang lightly from the tree, landed on his feet with his knees bent, and straightened up. Then he turned and offered his arms to his sister.

"I can get down, myself," she reminded him. She climbed down, as Nathan had done, by digging her fingers into knotholes, and clinging with her bare feet like a monkey. She reached the ground with barely a scrape and stood beside her brother.

"Come on," Jackson told her.

Mama was at the kitchen table, shaping dough to a blue ceramic pie dish. She spooned in a filling of fresh sliced peaches, sugar and syrup. Then she spread the top crust delicately over the whole thing. The crust didn't break, and she sighed with relief. Next, she pressed the tines of a fork into the outer edge of the dough, while briskly turning the dish with her left hand. This made a decorative crinkle in the border of the pie crust, and at the same time sealed it securely.

She glanced up, without pausing in her work, as Maggie and Jackson came in the back door.

"You wanted me, Mama?" Maggie asked meekly.

"I need you to fix the potatoes for supper. There's a bowl by the sink," Martha said, nodding in that direction. "Wash them and slice them up in there. After you peel 'em."

Maggie and Jackson exchanged a look.

"Yes, ma'am," Maggie breathed, relieved.

Jackson picked up a scrap of pie dough from the table and dropped it into his open mouth. He liked the taste of raw flour. He would have eaten the whole uncooked crust if he could get away with it.

"You need me for anything, Mama?" he said.

"What, now that you're done looking after Nathan?" she said tartly.

His eyes widened. "Momma! I totally forgot Nathan. I *was* watching him, Mama, until a little while ago."

She nodded tersely. "Well, he's upstairs now. I sent him to get his bath early."

"Sorry, Mama," Jackson murmured, genuinely remorseful.

"Mm. Well, if you want to be helpful, go look in on dad's Grandma. Let her know supper will be ready in about an hour, and ask if she needs anything meanwhile."

Jackson balked. "I could—I could do the potatoes and Maggie could check on Grandma."

"I'm peeling the potatoes," Maggie warned, hugging the bowl territorially to her chest.

"Mae is nothing for you to be afraid of, Jackson," Martha said reasonably. "We all might as well learn to be comfortable with her, she's going to be with us for some time to come yet."

"I'm not afraid," Jackson said, frowning. He cast an annoyed look at his little sister. "I just figured taking care of old ladies was sort of a girl thing, that's all."

"It's a family thing," Mama said firmly. "And don't be calling her an old lady."

"Well, ain't she?"

"Jackson, you are trying my patience."

"I'm gone," he promised, ruefully heading for the front bedroom, which now belonged to Mae.

"Come on," Iris said to Maggie that night, after supper. "I'm to put you to bed tonight, Mama said."

She took the girl's thin wrist in her hand and pulled her up the stairs.

"It's early," Maggie protested. "It's still light."

"Well, I got things to do. So you got to go on to bed now, you understand?"

Maggie followed her older sister up the stairs, frowning.

"I want Mama to put me to bed."

"I swear, if you don't sound like a puny little baby," Iris exclaimed, annoyed. "In the first place, you are old enough you ought to be putting your own self to bed, and that's for sure. In the second place, Mama is busy with the old lady. And that there is something you might as well get used to!"

The upstairs bedroom was dim. The light outside was falling. Iris turned on the lamp beside her bed, opened Maggie's dresser drawer, and shuffled through the tangled clothes, searching for a nightgown.

"There," she said, tossing a nondescript garment onto the bed. "Put that on."

Maggie shucked off her clothes obediently and slid into the pale cotton gown. She stood, barefoot, watching as her big sister leaned close to the mirror, one eye shut. She then smeared color from a little tube over her eye-lid.

"You goin' off with Albert tonight?" Maggie asked.

"Go wash your face and comb your hair," Iris answered.

Maggie went into the one bathroom which the whole family begrudgingly shared. She stood in front of the small bathroom mirror.

It was an old mirror, spotted around the edges, and only as big as the medicine cabinet door to which it was attached. But she could see her face in it.

Someone had left a small pile of copper-colored bobbie pins lying on the sink. Maggie picked up two and pinned the bangs back at her temples, to keep them from getting soapy. She dabbed at her face with a washcloth which she found wadded up, still wet from Nathan's bath.

Maggie studied her face in the splotchy mirror. It was curious the change that two ordinary bobbie pins made in her appearance. With the hair drawn back from her face, Maggie's thin cheeks looked fuller. Her eyes appeared bigger and brighter.

She left the bobbie pins in place and went back to her bedroom to show her sister.

Iris was sitting on her bed, polishing her nails. The room smelled strongly of nail enamel. She glanced up and saw Maggie standing in the doorway. She paused with the tiny brush suspended over her thumbnail, and looked hard at the child.

"What'd you do to your bangs?" she said, mildly suspicious.

"Pinned 'em back."

Iris polished the nail she had begun and then put the brush back in the little bottle. "It looks kind of nice," she admitted. "You don't look so much like an orphaned ragamuffin."

Maggie came in and sat on the bed beside her sister.

"Want some gum?" Iris offered. Maggie shook her head no. Her sister put a wad in her own mouth and chewed it vigorously. As soon as it was well-moistened, she began blowing tiny bubbles inside her mouth and popping them against her teeth.

"You and Albert going off somewhere?" Maggie inquired again as Iris resumed polishing her nails.

Iris popped her gum. "You know I got to work tonight," she said, half-scolding. She eyed her little sister carefully.

"Oh."

Iris smiled faintly, satisfied. "C'mere. If you hold real still, I'll paint your nails for you."

Maggie did not especially want her nails painted. But this extraordinary offer from her big sister could scarcely be turned down. She moved closer and yielded her hand to Iris.

Iris frowned. "Child, don't you ever wash your hands?"

"Me and Jackson went diggin' for worms," Maggie explained.

Iris nodded grimly. "I ought to have known."

Nevertheless, she smoothed polish onto her sister's small nails. Maggie watched in fascination the tiny black brush spreading bright, wet color.

"You should do your hair pinned like that when school starts back," Iris suggested. "With your nails done, and your hair fixed, why, you'd just be downright sassy."

"For real?" Maggie asked with wonderment, spreading her fingers to admire the coral-colored polish, while Iris began on her other hand.

Iris grinned and popped her gum. "Don't wiggle," she said.

The second day after Mae Burnett's arrival, Iris was assigned, despite vehement protests, to take her great-grandmother for a walk. Mae's doctor had ordered this daily exercise in hopes of Mae regaining some part of the skills and strengths she had lost during the stroke.

Mid-afternoon, with Martha standing peremptorily at her side, Iris pushed the door half-open with a simultaneous light tap.

"You in there?" she mumbled, peeking into the room.

Mae was in her rocking chair, dozing, her head bent down.

Iris closed the door and turned to her mother. "She's asleep," she announced cursorily as she started for the stairs.

"You just hold on there, young lady. Grandma Mae naps off and on. I'll see if she's sound asleep or not. Don't you go anywhere."

Mama entered the room quietly. In moments she was back. "She's awake," she notified Iris with an adamant nod.

Martha went back to the kitchen, leaving the two to work it out for themselves.

Iris reluctantly entered her grandma's bedroom.

It was true. Mae was awake, drowsily, still seated in the rocker.

"I'm s'posed to take you out for your walk," the girl informed the sleepy, unsuspecting woman with an audible sigh of discontent.

Mae looked at her through puzzled eyes, not making any move to get up.

Iris grasped the stainless steel walker with its rubber grips and set it down with a thud directly in front of her great-grandmother. "Here ya go." She blew a visible bubble with her gum and popped it loudly. "I reckon you know how this contraption works. I don't."

Mae just stared at the girl for a split second. She was taken aback by the bossiness. At the same time, she liked to see some spirit in a child. A sassy girl like this she didn't have to be so careful of. Not like fragile little Maggie.

Mae gave Iris a pleasant smile.

The girl's eyebrows shot up.

"What're you grinnin' about?" she asked suspiciously. "You *want* to go walkin'? I thought I was gonna have to drag you."

By way of answer, Mae pushed herself up out of the chair and, holding tightly to the walker, stood up and took a step.

"Well, all right," Iris approved. "Let's get this show on the road!"

Laboriously Mae picked up the walker a half-inch, moved it, and steadied her weight on it. Then she repeated the process. Again—and again, until she finally reached the door.

Iris stared, dumbfounded.

"Have mercy! Ma'am, that thing's more work than it's worth! Here," she commanded, linking her arm through Mae's. She pushed the walker off to one side.

"Now, I'm strong, and I'm not gonna let you fall," Iris said firmly. "So don't turn into a fraidy-cat on me, okay? We can do this. If we take that thing along we'll be done maybe by breakfast tomorrow!"

Mae gave a small laugh. It was almost soundless—just a squeaky inward rush of air. The awkward sound caught Iris off guard.

"Is that all the better you can laugh?" the girl said, unconsciously making a face. "I mean—"

Mae nodded.

Iris was silent for a long moment, studying Mae's face. "What's the matter with you? You got something wrong with your voice, too?"

Mae nodded again.

"Well, I'll be," Iris muttered. "Nobody bothered to tell me that. Nobody tells me *anything* around here. Except, Iris do this, Iris do that, Iris be home by ten, Iris take the old lady for a walk, Iris—I mean—" the girl blushed. "I didn't mean—umm—"

She still stood with Mae's arm through her own. She was suddenly acutely self-conscious. "I didn't mean to sound so—well—whatever I sounded. I'm sorry, hear?"

Mae just looked at her, mildly stunned by the outburst.

Isis said, "You *can* hear, can't you?".

At this, the older woman laughed again. She couldn't help herself. The same choked inrush of air which was all the stroke had left of her laughter. She gave Iris's arm a friendly squeeze and nodded.

Iris's face was flushed with embarrassment. "Oh well," she mumbled, chagrined. "I guess we'll learn each other as we go. Come on, then." Iris held her great-grandmother's arm snugly. "Don't worry, I got you."

They made their way with surprising ease through the living room and, more slowly, down the porch steps. Soon they were strolling in the small, neglected garden.

"I sure didn't know you couldn't talk," Iris ruminated mildly. Mae shrugged, as if to say it's all right.

"What do you mean—*shrug*? Didn't the doctor say you could regain some of your abilities? Isn't that how come we're out here practicing walking?"

Mae smiled politely.

"Well, you're walking real good, ma'am," Iris encouraged her. "And you had to learn how to do that again, right? That's what my mama *did* tell me."

The smile widened. Mae liked this girl. She liked her style.

"So you can learn how to talk again, too," Iris insisted. She looked at her great-grandmother's gentle face for a long minute and made a decision.

"I'll help you. School's out and I got time. If we both work at it, I believe we can do it."

Overhead a tiny brown bird burst into melodious song. Iris pointed, wanting Mae to notice.

"Hear that? You'll hear him lots. He hangs around the yard. I bet you could say 'bird.' What you reckon?"

Mae waved her hand no.

"Aw, come on. Be a sport. Just try."

Another shake of the head.

"Please?" Iris wheedled, nudging her gently as they walked. "Pretty please? Grandma?"

The grandmother smiled, in spite of herself.

"There you go," Iris encouraged. "That's the spirit. Bird. Buurrrdd. Just try—I won't tell anybody if you can't do it. But please try. For me?"

Mae hesitated.

"Grandma?" Iris cajoled.

Mae concentrated. Her lips formed carefully, but she made no sound.

Iris imitated her grandmother's poised lips. "Buh," Iris said, narrowing it down to the first consonant sound. "Buh."

Mae shook her head so pitifully that Iris was sorry for her. She put one arm around the fragile lady's shoulder.

"That's okay." Iris forced herself to smile. "We'll work on it some more next time we walk."

Martha watched them from the living room window. She mused quietly, "Just when I think I know my children, one or another of 'em takes my breath away."

"You talking to me, Mama?" Jackson asked. He looked up from his notebook, pencil in hand. Civil War library books and various sketches were spread out over half the kitchen table.

"No, son," she answered tenderly. "Just thinking out loud. You go ahead with your drawing. I'll say no more."

She turned away from the window with a familiar pang. Rare, glowing moments like this somehow made Reuben's absence more painful. It was always so.

After that first day of walking together, Iris didn't try again right away to make her grandmother talk. It seemed to dishearten her so. They walked together and Iris talked and Mae listened, often smiling. Before many days passed, they had actually become friends. They developed the habit of pausing to sit on the white wrought iron bench in the one-time garden, to let Mae catch her breath. She was constantly short of breath, Iris learned. And she learned something else. If Mae really tried she could whisper a few rushed syllables at a time until she got tired. Then nothing would come. Iris listened closely and carefully when her grandmother expressed any vocal sound that resembled words. She began to learn how to hear her.

Mama still watched them through the window for a moment here and there, and shook her head, marveling.

Tuesday evening Mama was clearing the supper table, with Mae doing her best to help, when a car pulled into the yard.

Mama heard the crunch of tires on gravel and came out of the kitchen with an apprehensive frown. She craned her neck to see out the front window without standing close enough to be seen.

"Oh, for heaven's sake!" she gasped, looking desperately around the living room. "It's the preacher! Sonny, get those newspapers up off the floor. Where's Nathan? Jackson, carry that there laundry basket upstairs for me, and tell your Daddy to put on his shoes and come down here. Where's Maggie?"

Maggie appeared, obediently, out of thin air. Mama took one look at her and called, "Iris—! Take this child upstairs and make her decent looking!"

"Can't be done," Iris remarked, coming in from the kitchen with an assessing glance in Maggie's direction.

There was a knock on the door.

"Hurry!" Mama hissed.

Iris grabbed her sister by the arm and pulled her out of sight.

Martha yanked off her apron, stuffed it under the sofa cushion, and patted her pinned up hair. She opened the front door with an air of quiet dignity.

"Preacher Lawson," she said respectfully. "Mighty nice to see you. This *is* a surprise! Come in the house."

Preacher Lawson held his hat in his hand and stepped politely inside the door. "I hope I'm not calling at a bad time?" he said a little apologetically. "I just wanted to stop by, check on you folks—"

Iris listened long enough to learn who had come to visit, then hustled her little sister up the stairs to the bathroom and took a washcloth to her face.

Maggie stood meekly submissive while her face was scrubbed to an angelic shine.

"Come on," Iris grumbled, dragging her to the bedroom. "We gotta find you a decent dress, if we can. Clean, anyhow."

Maggie slid into a cotton print shift. Iris pulled her over to the bed and began brushing her hair vigorously.

"It needs washing," Iris declared. "I wouldn't be caught dead with hair as dirty as this. What makes you want to be such a little raggymuffin, anyhow?"

Maggie crossed over to her dresser and rummaged until she found a folded piece of paper. This she handed to her sister. She said timidly, "Bethy Lawson gave me this. The day school let out. From her dad. I was—supposed to give it to Mama."

Iris frowned. She took the note in her hand and read,

"I'd like to come by to visit a little with you folks
around seven Tuesday week. I would have called, but

knowing you don't have a phone, I'm sending word by...
yadda, yadda....faithfully..."

Iris gave her little sister an exasperated look. "Oh, wonderful."

"I forgot until—"

"Yeah, I know. Until you heard the preacher knocking on the door." Iris rolled her eyes. She gave the girl's hair a final sweep with the brush. "Well, don't say nothing about it now, for heaven's sake. Mama'll wear you out, and who could blame her? Come on," she sighed, leading the way downstairs. "You don't look very spruce, but that's the best I can do."

"I'm sorry." Maggie looked into her sister's face.

"It's not your fault so much, Muffin. If we owned a phone..."

Iris continued her discontented discourse under her breath, all the way down the stairs.

The family rarely gathered all together in the living room, and they virtually never had company. The room looked over-full and unnatural to Maggie.

Sonny and Jackson were standing together, awkwardly, by the window. Lester sat straight and stiff in the brown chair. Beside him Mama sat solemnly in a straight chair from the kitchen, holding Nathan against her side so she could pinch him, unseen, should the need arise.

Only Mae, sitting on the sofa beside the preacher, seemed comfortable with the visit.

Yet the conversation went all around her, without actually including her. There was not much choice. After a perfunctory welcome and a few questions which Mae could answer by nodding or shaking her head, the preacher and Lester had fallen into talking about sports. Sonny quickly joined in. Mama was primly silent.

Iris's brow frowned slightly. She pointed Maggie toward the window, whispering for her to go stand with her brothers.

Iris seated herself on the arm of the sofa and put a hand on her great-grandmother's shoulder.

"Grandma used to sing in the choir, back at her church in Kentucky," she informed Preacher Lawson, the first instant there was a lapse in the sports conversation.

"Is that so?" he said, turning in Mae's direction to indicate interest. "What church was that, Mrs. Burnett?"

The older lady smiled with a nod. Then she tapped her fingers against her lips and shook her head, apologetically.

Iris sat up straight. "She means that she can't talk, but she can. You can too talk," Iris insisted, addressing her grandmother. "She *can* talk—a little—Preacher Lawson. She had a stroke, you know, but—"

"No," Mae murmured to silence her, patting her hand affectionately.

Preacher Lawson bent his head a little to look into Mae's face. "I didn't mean to ignore you," he said kindly. "Please forgive me. I had heard about your stroke, yes. I didn't know how extensive the damage was, and I didn't want to press."

Mae nodded reassuringly.

"We've been working at it," Iris explained, eagerly. "In the afternoon—"

"Iris," Lester said sternly, calling her down.

Preacher Lawson intervened. "No, please. I'm very much interested."

Iris cast her father a questioning glance, but he refused to meet her gaze.

"Can we show you something?" she asked tentatively.

"By all means. Please do," said the preacher.

"Watch this," Iris said, her voice full of promise. She turned to Mae. "Remember how to say bird?"

Mae shook her head again, touching her lips.

"Bird," Iris modeled for her again, slowly.

Mae lowered her eyes, embarrassed, but unwilling to let Iris down. Very softly she whispered, "Burr."

Iris sat up and clapped her hands together. "Yes! See?"

Preacher Lawson took Mae's hand in his and held it kindly. "I can see why you are making progress," he told her. "You have an enthusiastic young helper, here, don't you?"

Mae nodded yes.

Abruptly, Lester stood up. "Appreciate you droppin' by, Preacher. I know you got other house calls to make. We won't hold you up no longer."

Martha looked at her husband in wide-eyed astonishment.

"I was just going to fix Preacher Lawson a plate," she stammered. Then floundering to regain her composure, she said to the minister, "We just got done eating, and there was mountains of food left over." This, of course, was not true. "Let me fix you something."

Preacher Lawson politely stood also, saying, "Thank you, Martha, that is surely kind of you, but I really do have to be going. This has been a real blessing to me. I hope to see you all, come Sunday."

He shook Lester's hand, patted Nathan on the head, spoke a brief prayer of benediction, and was gone.

Mama said to Mae, "I know you must be exhausted. Iris, help her back to her room."

"Yes'm," Iris said.

As soon as they were gone, Martha looked at her husband with eyes of fire. "That I should live to see the day—!" she declared in an infuriated whisper "—my own husband run the preacher off!"

Lester was equally angry. "Iris had no business to go trying to show Grandma off like that, like she was a baby just learning to talk or something! Made me ashamed! I aim to speak to her about it, too."

Martha folded her arms, drawing herself up with quiet dignity. "Lester. Your grandma has brought out something good in that girl that I never guessed was there. I've watched them together. If you go fussing at Iris for what she done just now, you'll destroy something you don't mean nor want to destroy. You'll do them both harm."

Lester frowned. "She embarrassed my grandmother."

"No, she embarrassed you. There's a big difference."

Lester cast an unsettled look in the direction of the front bedroom. Iris was still in there, helping Mae get dressed for bed and settled in. He looked back at his wife stonily.

"I'm goin' back out and work some overtime in the fields. Pickin'. While there's still light."

"Fine." With arms resolutely still folded, Martha watched him go. Then, sighing, she pulled her apron out from under the sofa cushion and tied it back around her waist. There were dozens of dishes still to be washed.

Sonny said, "Don't worry, Mama. He won't say nothing."

"Don't none of you all say anything either," she warned the children, looking from Sonny and Jackson to Maggie. "And I mean it." She gripped Nathan by his shoulder and gave him a little shake. "You understand me? I'll whup you silly if you say one word about this."

Nathan understood.

"Now hush," she whispered severely, as Iris came out of the bedroom.

"Mama," the girl said, "Did it seem to you the preacher left in a mighty hurry? He didn't even hardly touch his coffee."

"I don't know," Martha said, flustered. "It took me by surprise too. Maybe he could tell he'd come at a bad time. Come help me with the dishes, Iris. I declare, I don't see why folks can't allow somebody some warning, one way or another, instead of just dropping in like that."

Maggie cast an uneasy glance toward her big sister. Iris, without batting an eye, said, "Maybe if we had a telephone, like decent, civilized people—"

"Nevermind," Mama sighed, heading back to the kitchen.

The snake in the woods held an increasing fascination for Jackson. He was determined to find it, determined to kill it.

The day after the preacher's visit he woke with this mission foremost in his mind. He worked extra hard all day to finish his chores. By early evening, he had done everything his mother could find for him to do. She told him he could go play.

Jackson was not naturally hostile to snakes. Neither was he, by nature, much of a hunter. But this snake had a wicked look about it that Jackson didn't like. He didn't want it loose in the woods where his little brother and sister played, and where he sometimes liked to fish. He had glimpsed the snake twice since the day he and Maggie first discovered it in the kudzu. That was three times too many, as he figured it.

Sonny was of the opinion that the snake had easily as much right to the woods, and probably more, than a bunch of loud-mouthed kids, and they ought to leave it alone. Jackson paid him no mind.

But now, on the verge of leaping down the back porch steps, Jackson halted suddenly, arrested by a subdued sound. A soft, sniffling sound, like someone with a mild cold.

There. He heard it again.

He turned back to the interior of the porch and looked in the direction from which the sound had come. An old mattress was kept in the far corner of the screened back porch—a place for the children to play or nap. On the edge of this mattress, half-hidden in shadow, Maggie sat huddled into a tight knot.

"Maggie?" Jackson said, taking a step toward her. She drew further, if possible, into the knot she had made of herself.

"Come on, now," her brother said in a reasonable voice.

"Go away," she mumbled.

Jackson sat down on the mattress, at the far end away from Maggie.

He glanced at her and then looked out at the deepening afternoon sky. He waited.

"You gonna tell me what happened?" he asked, finally.

Silence.

After a few minutes, he tried again. "Come on, Maggie. What got you to crying?"

"I'm not crying," she said distinctly, through the space between her crossed arms.

"You were crying before."

"Go away. Please."

Jackson frowned. He stood up. "Well, all right. I'll go. I'm fixin' to go hunt that big snake in the woods, anyhow."

No answer.

He pushed open the screen and bounded down the steps and across the back yard. But he didn't actually go into the woods. He only kicked around the edges a little, in a dissatisfied way. After a while he came back up on the porch, and sat down in one of the rockers. He rocked, looking out at the sky, which was beginning to glow in magenta and amber.

Maggie, meanwhile, had unknotted herself and sat leaning back against the house with her legs stretched out on the discarded mattress.

She picked at her fingernails. It was an unconscious habit she had when nervous or upset. Sometimes she tore at her nails until they bled, and then, at night, her fingertips throbbed and kept her awake.

Jackson knew without looking at her what she was doing. He said, "Quit messin' with your nails, girl."

Maggie sat up on the mattress and looked over at her brother. "Did you find the snake?" she asked.

He shook his head. "Not today."

There was a pause.

Jackson said, "What happened, Maggie? What were you crying about, awhile ago?"

Maggie sighed. She was fully in control of herself now. She answered in a monotone. "Nathan killed my cricket. I found it—what was left of it. He smushed the band-aid box, too."

"You sure it was Nathan?" her brother wanted to know.

"Who else?" she pointed out with uncharacteristic logic. "Besides, I asked him, and he said maybe yes, maybe no. And he stuck out his tongue at me."

Jackson's face lost all expression. His breathing quickened. "D'you tell Mama?" he asked her, struggling to conceal his anger.

Maggie nodded tiredly. "She said she was measuring things for a recipe and —not to—confuse her," Maggie answered, working to remember Mama's exact words. "Said she didn't have time right now for—our foolishness."

Jackson stood up abruptly.

Maggie raised her head, questioning. "Where you goin'?"

Her brother left without a word.

A wave of self-pity swept over Maggie. Nobody seemed to care about her troubles. First Mama, and now Jackson. Tears rimmed her eyes again, and she blotted them with the hem of her dress.

Suddenly, from deep inside the house she heard some kind of noisy confusion. She looked toward the door apprehensively. The disturbance moved into the kitchen, with considerable scuffling and muffled protest. There was a sudden, loud smack that made Maggie jump. Nathan's voice raised in a siren-like wail, but a mumbled threat, followed by a second slap, shut him up.

Jackson appeared in the doorway, holding his little brother by the shirt collar. Nathan's eyes were full of furious tears. His left cheek was flushed deep pink.

"Tell her," Jackson commanded, pushing the child toward Maggie.

Nathan puffed up like a bandy rooster, his face a solid frown. "I'm sorry I kilt your stupid old---"

Jackson jerked his collar.

"Ow! Quit!"

"Say it right."

Nathan tugged at his collar and pronounced in a sulky tone, "I'm sorry I kilt your cricket, Maggie."

Maggie raised questioning eyes to Jackson's face. "Do I have to say it's all right?"

"No, you do not," Jackson said vehemently. "'Cause it's not all right. You don't have to say nothin'."

He gave Nathan a shove toward the kitchen. "Go on, get out of here."

Nathan ran inside the house, hollering for his mother.

Jackson sat back down in the rocking chair, looking soberly out at the rose-colored sky.

Sitting on the mattress, Maggie leaned forward, folded her hands across her knees and rested her chin on them. Out of the corner of her eye she looked gratefully at her brother.

Quietly she said, " That's just Nathan. He's mean."

Jackson shook his head. "He knows better. Ought to, anyhow."

The last of the sun had slipped below the tree tops, leaving the world noticeably darker. The two children watched without speaking as the outline of the hills and woods began to turn an indistinct purplish-grey.

It didn't take long for Martha to appear in the lighted doorway.

"Jackson," she said gravely, "your little brother tells me you slapped him."

"I did," Jackson said, without looking around.

Martha folded her arms. "I can see that you did; his face is as red as pickled beets."

"Well, you wouldn't do nothing," Jackson grumbled. "He just—"

"Hold on there, young man," Martha said sternly. "You will turn around and look at me when you talk to me. And show some respect."

Jackson pressed his lips together, annoyed. But he did what he was told. "Nathan took Maggie's cricket and killed it, just for meanness. All I did was make him apologize. Somebody ought to beat the devil out of him."

Martha said cooly, "Well, *somebody* better not be you."

Jackson looked back out at the darkening sky.

His mother studied the back of his head for an instant. Then she came up behind his chair, took a firm grip on his hair, and bent his head back so that he had to look up at her.

"I said—if there's to be any devil-beating around this house, that's up to me or your Daddy," she repeated quietly. "Nobody else. You understand me?"

He gave her a begrudging "Yes, ma'am."

Mama went back into the house, without so much as a word to Maggie.

Jackson scowled. He smoothed his hair down and stared at the sky, without seeing it.

Maggie looked at him tentatively.

For some time, neither of them spoke.

It was dark, now, and in the light from the kitchen door they were only silhouettes. Black figures against a near-black background.

Finally, with admiration, Maggie murmured, "You took up for me."

"So quit tearing up your fingernails."

The next morning, Jackson was up before dawn. The weather was cool and invigorating. He had a half-bucketful of worms that he had dug the afternoon before, with Maggie and Nathan's help. He was supposed to wake both children early, so they could go with him. But he had not known that he, himself would wake an hour before first light.

He had dressed in the dark and slipped downstairs without a sound. He would have at least a half-hour to fish in solitude, he figured, without the frustration of having to shush Nathan and try to keep Maggie from wading and scaring the fish. He would come back for them, then.

By flashlight, he made his way carefully to the creek. Once there, he baited his hook, tossed it into the deepest water, and sat on a cold rock to wait. Maggie awoke not long after Jackson left the house. She was up and dressed without disturbing Iris. She crept down to the back porch and waited, thinking Jackson was still asleep.

It was chilly on the porch, and she had not brought her sweater. She rubbed her arms briskly and watched the crevice of pale pink that slowly lighted the eastern sky.

Maggie was grateful for this rare moment of outdoor solitude. She soaked in the peace of the early morning, the sweet cacophony of the birds singing, and the blessedness of no words being spoken.

A small, questioning sound broke into Maggie's thoughts. A sound so minute that she was not entirely sure she had heard it. She stepped down from the porch and listened intently.

The sound came again, this time much nearer. Maggie stooped deeply down and peered into the darkness under the porch steps.

Two tiny green eyes peered back at her. The sound was repeated—a faint, frightened little mew.

"It's a kitten," Maggie whispered, awed. She beckoned with her fingers. "Come here, kitty. I won't hurt you."

The kitten blinked its eyes nervously. It would not come.

Maggie sat down on the ground. She thought of reaching under the porch to pull the kitten out. But she knew that would only frighten it more. She settled herself patiently to wait.

Suddenly she saw Jackson burst wildly out of the woods, racing headlong for the house.

She had been so sure he was upstairs still asleep, she could scarcely process this new turn of events.

She jumped to her feet, staring.

"Get out the way," Jackson ordered, pushing past her. He took the steps in one mighty leap.

"What is it? What's the matter?" Maggie cried in alarm.

Jackson was in the house only an instant. He reappeared with his father's rifle under one arm. He paused long enough to say excitedly, "I seen that evil snake again, smack dab over the fishing hole. I hooked a fish and when I was pulling it in, I looked up—and there that snake was, looped around a tree branch, practically on top of me, with his wicked-looking old head hanging down and his fangs fluttering like red fire. This time I'm gonna get him!"

He started for the woods and Maggie followed, trembling, running, trying to keep up. She snatched at his sleeve. "We can't none of us touch Daddy's gun," she warned him.

"Let go me," Jackson snapped. He shook himself loose and broke for the edge of the woods, at a full run.

Maggie hugged herself against the morning chill. She was trembling visibly now. Her eyes strained toward the woods. She heard a sleepy owl call, and the faint murmurs of waking creatures. Gentle sounds, accompanying the serene light of a new-born day.

She remembered the frightened kitten, and turned back to the porch steps. The tiny cat was right where she had left it. It had not moved at all.

"Kitty?" she tried again, in the mildest of tones. "Come, kitty-kitty?"

Suddenly the harsh report of Lester's gun exploded through the quiet morning air. Maggie was so startled by the violent sound that her whole body jolted.

There followed a moment—just an instant—of deceptive stillness, as if everything were perfectly normal and peaceful again.

Then Maggie heard footsteps, heavy but quick, on the stairs inside the house. She turned in time to see Lester lunge out the back door, his eyes dark with sleep, his hair matted and disheveled. He had not taken time to put on either shoes or a shirt, and wore only his khaki work pants.

"I heard gunfire—" he said harshly to Maggie, as if it were somehow her fault.

She opened her mouth, but not a sound would come out.

Mama, wrapped in her faded pink chenille bathrobe, appeared in the kitchen doorway, with Nathan peeping out from behind her.

"Lester, what is it?" she said tremulously.

"Don't know," he answered brusquely. "But I aim to find out."

He started across the backyard with purposeful strides.

At the same moment, Jackson emerged from the woods, jogging triumphantly toward the house.

When he saw his father, his steps slowed.

Lester took one look at the rifle in the boy's hand and needed no explanation.

He reached the place where Jackson stood, jerked the gun away from him and emptied out the remaining shells. He bent down and laid the gun in the grass.

Jackson watched him warily. "Daddy—" he began.

Swift as lightning, Lester straightened up, drew back his arm and struck the boy a furious blow with his fist.

Jackson staggered backward, lost his balance, and fell sprawling in the grass.

Watching from the kitchen doorway, Martha gave a little involuntary cry, and quickly pressed her hand to her mouth to stifle it.

Recovering her composure, she said without emotion, "You children come on back inside." She turned and went into the house, and Nathan followed her. "Maggie?" she called back.

But Maggie stood riveted, biting and chewing her hand, staring in helpless silence at the scene before her.

Jackson made no attempt to get up. He lay propped on one elbow, his eyes fixed on his father's face, not even attempting to wipe away the blood that spilled from his nose and lip.

Lester stood with his legs spread wide, balanced, his fist still clenched. When he spoke, his voice was hard. "You know better'n to take my rifle like that. Nobody is allowed to touch that gun but me."

Jackson cleared his throat. "Yes, sir."

"Get up on your feet, then, like a man."

Jackson swallowed hard. He pushed himself to his knees and stood up slowly, dreading that his father was going to hit him a second time.

But Lester bent slowly and picked up the gun. He held it under his arm, barrel down, and looked at his son long and hard.

"I don't expect us to have this conversation again, y'understand?"

Jackson nodded ruefully.

"All right then." Lester said in a notably subdued voice. He waited. His hand, no longer a fist, was trembling. The initial rage had washed out of him in an instant at the sight of his son's face, splotched with blood and already beginning to swell. But he couldn't apologize, as if he had been wrong. As if what the boy had done was not so serious after all. He sought for conciliatory words, struggling. This was, after all, the finest of his sons, the one who never gave him any trouble. Lester silently cursed his own quick temper. He started to walk away, and then turned back.

Jackson stiffened with apprehension. His father saw it and was ashamed. He stayed back several arm's length, not to frighten him further.

"Jackson," he said slowly, quietly. He paused, not finding words. He studied the boy's face. There was no rebellion in his demeanor, no anger. Only the same expression in his eyes that he saw all too often in Maggie's.

Lester couldn't bear to see that look in his son's eyes, too. He averted his gaze, focusing on the sky, just now turning amber and pink with the sunrise. The birds had resumed their morning jubilee, not comprehending the scene that had taken place beneath them. Lester sighed deeply.

"Son," he began again, in a quieted voice. "It's a natural thing, I reckon, for a southern boy to want to hunt. I guess it's time I taught you how. If you'll wait until peach season is over, I'll show you how to use a gun proper. Teach you to hunt, if that's what you want. But you'll have to wait. And don't mess with my gun in the meantime."

Jackson whispered, "Yes, sir." He wanted to clarify that he didn't care about hunting, he had just wanted that particular snake out of the way. But he dared not attempt to explain.

Lester nodded sorrowfully. He turned and walked back to the house, brushing past Maggie without acknowledging her presence. He mounted the sagging porch steps heavily and disappeared into the kitchen.

Martha was standing just inside the door, waiting.

"Lester—" she murmured in gentle reproach.

"You don't have to say it," he told her, moving past without meeting her gaze. "I already know."

Outside, Maggie watched her brother through a blur of tears.

Jackson stood dazed, wiping his face against his arm, shaking his head a little and testing his jaw. His hand was crimson with blood from his nose and lip. He blotted it with his shirt tail.

Slowly, unsteadily, he walked toward the back porch.

When he came to where Maggie stood he stopped, arrested by the stricken expression in her eyes.

"You don't need to be lookin' at me like that," he told her. "I'm okay. It's just blood, is all. I ain't dead or nothing."

The child could only stare at him in mute dismay.

"Hey," he said with a small, painful attempt at a grin. "I kilt that snake, anyhow."

That night, Martha dreamed about Reuben. It was a frightening dream—one of those where some unclear horror lurks at the edges of what should have been a simple family supper. She woke gasping for breath.

"Lester," she whispered, shaking him awake. "I had a bad dream. Hold me."

Les rolled over and encircled her with his arm. "What got you so scared, girl?" he asked, kissing her ear.

"We were having supper and Reu—"

"That's all I need to hear. I see where this is headed."

"He wasn't here."

"He isn't here. That's a fact, not a nightmare."

"But—"

"You know better than to talk about him. Go back to sleep."

Martha couldn't stand Les being mad at her when she was so afraid. She did what she had long known to do when she needed her husband. She kissed his neck, then his lips. He returned the kiss willingly. Truth was, they seldom had time, privacy or energy to make love anymore. Lester reached under the covers and ran his hand across her smooth thigh.

It was only a dream with no meaning, Martha forced herself to believe. Here in her arms, she held what was the truth. It comforted her. She found herself murmuring words she had not spoken in a good while: "Lester, I love you." And hearing them returned.

The two fell back to sleep wrapped in a grateful embrace.

There was rain the next day. It stopped in early afternoon, and the evening was languid and fragrant. The front door was open, letting the sweet summer air fill the house.

In the living room, Jackson sat sideways in the over-stuffed chair, sketching on a notepad. On the floor beside him, sharing the light from the floor lamp, Maggie lay on her stomach, with her chin on her arms, reading the beginner level book which she had checked out of the school library and never remembered to return, despite notices received.

Sonny had completed a short pick-up and delivery run and was home for the weekend, catching up on five days of newspapers. Now and then he interrupted the children's concentration by reading out loud something that he considered of special interest.

Martha was just coming downstairs from getting Nathan to bed, when Lester's car belatedly pulled up in the yard.

"You're home," Martha said, relieved, as her husband strode through the door. "I've kept your supper warm—with the rain I thought you'd be home early—" her voice trailed off apprehensively as she took in the expression on his face.

Lester crossed the room to where Maggie lay and pulled her up off the floor by one arm.

"Daddy—" the girl entreated, trying to ease his painful grip just below her shoulder.

"You hush," Lester said severely.

He turned to Martha, explaining: "I got a message at work, telling me to come by the Campobello school district office." His voice was intense with barely controlled anger. "Maggie's teacher and principal were there. Wanted to know why she didn't never bring her signed report card back in before the last day of school."

Jackson swung his feet down and sat up in the chair. He looked at his mother.

"Oh, my! Lester, I forgot all about it," she gasped. "What with one thing and another. Mercy, what must that teacher think of us? I don't even remember now what I done with it, Lester."

"Don't matter. Teacher's got records of everything at the school house. She showed me. She asked me did I know that Maggie was failin' in school? And was I aware that she was being held back to fourth grade again next year?"

He was looking at Maggie, now, his face bitterly hard.

"I told her no ma'am," Lester continued, "that's the first I've heard tell of it. She asked me, did I not see the report card? I said no ma'am, I assuredly did not."

"Oh, Les," Martha sighed, one hand on her forehead.

"I ain't finished," he told her. "There's more. Teacher told me she has done her best to work with Maggie, tried to help her—kept her in from recess and give her extra work for practice. She said the problem was, Maggie don't seem to care if she does good or not. Maggie don't take a interest, she said, don't pay attention. That's what she said. Maggie don't pay attention, and don't try."

An awful silence fell over the room. Maggie stared down at the floor, shivering.

"You come with me," Lester told her, pulling her by the arm.

Jackson sprang to his feet. "Daddy, that teacher, that Mrs. Sanders, she's wrong," he said hoarsely. He pointed to the library book lying open in the floor. "Look there. Maggie was studying a book from school when—"

Lester said, "You stay out of it, boy. This is nothing to do with you."

He pushed Maggie ahead of him, up the stairs.

Sonny, looking after them, gave a low whistle. "She's in for it now," he said with a half-grin, going back to his paper.

"Mama, go up," Jackson implored. "Talk to him."

Martha shook her head tiredly. "Wouldn't do no good." Her eyes turned to the stairway and she rubbed the back of her neck with a sigh. "And I had just this minute got Nathan to sleep," she murmured.

Furious, Jackson flung himself out the front door, letting the screen bang shut behind him.

The night air was cool. Already the crickets were chirping, and from the distant lake came the faintly noisy intermittent quacking of ducks.

Half-way across the front yard, Jackson turned and looked up at the window of Maggie's bedroom. He saw the light come on, and through the open window, he heard his father's angry voice.

The boy took off, racing across the field, tripping over the uneven dirt and stubby dried stalks, falling and righting himself, and hurrying on.

The noises from the house followed him like phantoms. He reached the woods, and continued to run as fast as he was able. But he couldn't run fast enough to escape the sound of the belt striking or his sister's terrified crying.

Jackson ran until he came at last to the small lake behind the neighbor's farm. There he threw himself onto the ground, lying on his back, with one arm folded over his face.

The ducks scurried splashing into the water, with squawks of protest at this intrusion. They drifted on the surface of the lake, swimming aimlessly to and fro, watching the boy suspiciously from a safe distance.

Angry tears burned in Jackson's eyes. One by one, they brimmed over and slid in silent misery down across his temples and into his hair. He made no effort to brush them away.

He had tried so hard to protect his little sister. And he had failed completely. As the long minutes passed, Jackson tried to think things through. Thinking logically sometimes helped him calm himself. This whole thing was partly his fault, he fretted, because he had never given the report card back to his mother after Nathan dropped it under the table. He had known he should. But he had feared the consequences for Maggie. Now it had all turned out worse than he imagined.

The tears flowed again, briefly. Well, he reasoned, there was no avoiding the fact that Maggie had failed fourth grade. Neither would there have been any way to soften his father's anger, regardless when or how this news reached him. It couldn't be helped. He had tried. But it was out of his hands. And it was not actually his fault. It was just what was bound to happen.

Stabilized somewhat by facing this reality, the boy began to breathe more evenly. By now maybe Maggie had fallen asleep. This thought also helped ease his agitation.

The boy's anger was soon spent and he became moody and morose. He let his mind wander aimlessly.

Summer nights were beautiful in the countryside of Spartanburg county. Jackson became aware of a musical chorus of frogs, sounds that under happier circumstances would have made him smile. The frogs were accompanied by tuneful crickets and shallow-splashing ripples at the lake's edge.

Jackson wiped the last of his tears away and opened his eyes.

Overhead, the black sky was washed with milky bands of starlight. The night was perfectly clear, and every star was brilliantly visible. The boy's thoughts drifted, mesmerized by the magnificence of the heavens. He identified the Big Dipper, and the constellation Orion. He saw a pattern of stars that formed a W. He knew that one, he chided himself. He thought hard and long, but could not remember its name, until he ceased trying. Then he slapped his forehead. "Cassiopeia," he said aloud. "Of course."

Jackson pushed himself up on his elbows and looked out over the lake.

The water was as black as the sky, but luminous, and in constant, gentle motion from the stirring of the ducks' webbed feet.

It was then that he saw it—pale lamp-light shining through the broken-paned windows of the old abandoned shack beyond the lake.

Jackson sat all the way up, squinting his eyes.

Someone was in that shack.

There was a thin stream of smoke coming up from the old, half-crumbled chimney. Someone was living there, Jackson realized, with a shock. Undoubtedly, someone who wished to keep his whereabouts unknown.

The mystery of it captivated Jackson. He pushed himself up into a half-crouch. His body was stiff from lying so long on the cool, hard ground.

Shielded by the dark, Jackson moved cautiously closer to the tiny cabin. He straightened himself and hid behind a large oak tree, watching.

Within the shack a figure moved past the square opening that had once been a window. Jackson wrinkled his nose at the acrid smell of fish frying. The figure moved again, and now he could see what looked like a very small wood stove.

Jackson took a deep breath and moved quickly, silently, to the very corner of the broken porch. He pressed himself against the uneven boards of the shack, inching his way closer to the open window. At last he reached it and, holding his breath, dared to look in.

The man at the stove had his back to Jackson.

He was young, thin, and unkempt—the red and grey plaid shirt he wore was both wrinkled and soiled. His dark brown hair hung in uneven locks, as if he had cut it himself, using dull scissors.

The man scraped at the fish in the black frying pan, turned it. Then, still unaware of the young boy watching from the window, he flipped the fish onto an old tin pie plate and sat at the table to eat.

For one brief moment, Jackson was able to get a clear look at the man's face.

He drew back from the window, stunned.

Part Three

It was late when Jackson got home that night. All the house was quiet.

He slipped soundlessly up the stairs to his sisters' room and cautiously pushed open the door.

Iris had been browsing through a romance magazine by flashlight, hidden under the bed covers. She turned the blinding beam of light straight into Jackson's face.

"Quit," he complained, thrusting his hand in front of his eyes.

"Jackson," she scolded in a whisper, sitting up. "You scared me half to death! I thought you had the good sense to knock before you come bustin' into somebody's room. Obviously not."

She put the flashlight under a corner of her bedsheet, so that it gave off only a soft, diffuse glow, like a nightlight.

Jackson said, "Is Maggie all right?"

"She's asleep, Einstein," Iris said, rolling her eyes. "Jackson, it's half-past eleven, for crying out loud. Go to bed."

"I didn't know," he replied defensively. "I didn't know it was that late. I just wanted to find out if Maggie is okay."

"Go to bed, will you?"

Jackson looked toward his little sister's bed, obscure in the shadows at the far end of the room. He glanced back at Iris, but she had already slid under the covers and returned to studying her magazine.

The boy hesitated, deliberating.

"Iris, I gotta talk to you," he said, making his decision.

"Go to bed" came a muffled reply.

"Iris—this is important. I mean it."

The seriousness of his tone made Iris emerge from her bedspread and look suspiciously at her brother's face.

"If this is some foolishness that could've waited until morning—" she threatened.

Jackson interrupted. "I saw our brother. I saw Reuben."

Iris was stunned into silence. For an instant her face was totally expressionless. Then her eyes narrowed.

"What do you mean—what are you talkin' about?" she demanded.

"He's staying in that old abandoned shack behind Johnson's Lake. I was down there tonight. I'm telling you, I saw him."

Iris dropped her magazine with a frown. "What in the world were you doing down at the lake, this time of night?"

"Never mind that. I saw lights inside the shack. And I snuck over there and looked in the window. I swear, it was Reuben."

Iris regarded him skeptically, her heart beating hard now. She was at a loss what to say. She stalled. "Do you even remember what Reuben looks like?"

"I do," Jackson said, bristling. "I was nine years old when he went away. You think I'm so stupid I can't remember my own brother's face for four and a half years? Look, if you want, I'll take you down there right now and show you."

Iris wrinkled her brows into a fierce frown. "No, I ain't going down to the lake at midnight in the pitch dark like a blamed fool! Besides, faces change in four years. Whoever it was you saw, he's like as not nobody we know or ever have known. Some homeless person, using Johnson's shed to hang out awhile."

"It was Reuben," Jackson insisted stubbornly. A cold chill ran down Iris's back. It *could* be Reuben, she knew. Somehow the thought frightened her.

"Let me think," Iris demanded, waving an impatient hand at her brother. Jackson waited.

"Tomorrow," Iris said decisively. " No, wait. I got to work tomorrow. Never mind—I'll be off at four. It'll still be light for hours. I'll go down there with you, soon as I get home. We'll go together. If it is Reuben, we'll bring him home."

"What'll we do then?"

"I don't know. We'll think of something. I ain't leaving no brother of mine to starve to death in an abandoned old shanty shack."

"Iris," Jackson said slowly. "What happened to Reuben? What'd he go to jail for?"

The girl leaned back against her pillows. "You not supposed to ask me about that," she said in a low voice. "I am not allowed to talk about it."

"He's my brother, too."

"So? That don't make me allowed to talk about it, if I ain't allowed to talk about it. Now does it?"

"Did he kill somebody, or what?" Jackson persisted.

Iris sat up, frowning furiously. "*No*, he didn't kill anybody! How can you even say such a horrible thing!"

"What did he do, then?" Jackson challenged.

Iris saw that he had set a trap for her. Her eyes narrowed. But there was a glint of respect in them, too.

She leaned forward conspiratorially.

"All right," she said in a whisper. "But if you let on that I told—I swear—"

"Deal," Jackson said without hesitation. He stuck out his hand and they shook on it.

"Reuben got linked up somehow with a couple of guys that were nothing but trouble from the word go," Iris confided in a whisper. "He quit school, got to where he didn't even come home nights. One of these guys, maybe more, had a gun. Late one Saturday night they held up a liquor store up town. This guy with the gun shot the store owner in the shoulder. Nobody got bad hurt," Iris emphasized. "But it was what they call armed robbery, because that one guy had a loaded gun and used it. And Reuben, since he was with them, he was guilty, too. That's the law."

Jackson breathed out an almost inaudible whistle. "That's bad."

Iris nodded. "He was going on twenty, then. So he was tried as an adult and sent down to the state prison."

Jackson was quiet for a long minute.

"Iris," he said at last, "what was Reuben like? I mean, before. I remember his face, but—I don't remember *him* much."

"Reuben was hard to know," Iris recalled pensively. "He kept to himself—you know, kind of like Maggie. Only, he wasn't scared of things—more like Sonny that way. But that was the only thing about him that bore any likeness to Sonny."

"He had dark hair like me," Jackson said, remembering the face he'd seen through the window.

Iris smiled a little. "Yeah, brown and straight and all the time in his eyes. He had a little bit of all of us in him, I reckon," she said, her voice softening. "Didn't talk much—he was like Daddy that way. He didn't hardly ever smile or laugh, same as Mama. And he could be—you know—kind of sweet, but at the same time he had a mean streak, too—just exactly like Nathan."

"How was he like you, then?" Jackson wanted to know.

Iris grinned. "Good-looking. Naturally."

There was a restless murmur from Maggie's bed.

Iris and Jackson were instantly silent and motionless. Iris turned the flashlight off. The room was dark except for a cloudy dusting of moonlight.

In a subdued whisper, Iris instructed her brother, "Go on to bed and get some sleep. If it *is* Reuben you saw in that shack, we'll find it out tomorrow."

Maggie was slow to get up the next day. She said her head ached, and she stayed in bed throughout the morning.

Jackson tried to persuade her to come down to lunch, but she was preoccupied with her doll, Nellie. Nellie had spent the better part of the last two years on a high shelf in the closet. But today Maggie had taken a renewed interest in her. She sat up in bed, straightening the doll's clothes, trying with her fingers to press the wrinkles out of the lace collar and make it lie flat again.

She ignored Jackson's presence entirely. With a sigh he left her alone.

It was mid-afternoon before Jackson tried again. By then Maggie was ready to come down and join the rest of the family. But she insisted on bringing her doll with her.

"That's fine," Jackson assured her. "Come on, let's go down to the creek or something. Let's figger out a way to catch those gone-in-a-lickety-split minnows of yours." He gave her a crooked grin, and she actually smiled a little in return, liking the lilting sound of his words.

They found Mama and Mae on the back porch seated in the two rocking chairs, shelling field peas.

"Well," said Martha. "Come on you two, pull up a chair and help us out."

"Naw, Mama, we're on our way—" a loud puttering noise drowned Jackson out.

Nathan lay on his side on the porch floor, indolently rolling an intricately built model of a yellow truck up and back, buzzing his lips to imitate the sound of a motor.

"That's my old truck," Jackson noticed with a frown.

His mother gave him a mild look. "Surely you don't still want to play with toy trucks, Jackson."

"'Course not!" The boy was so humiliated that his cheeks flushed bronze. "But I didn't never say *he* could have it."

126

"Well, I did," returned his mother. "Here." She held out a bowl to him, and a handful of pea pods.

"But I *built* that model truck, Mama—it's mine 'cause Sonny gave me the kit for my birthday a couple years ago, and he helped me put it together and paint it and put on the decals and everything."

"All the same, you've outgrown it." Mama looked up at him from under a raised eyebrow, as if to dare him to disagree. She held the bowl of pea pods out to him.

"Can't," he said, taking a step backward.

"I'd like to know why not?"

"I got plans, Mama," he protested, folding his arms.

"What plans?" she asked.

Maggie appeared in the doorway, wearing one of her old play dresses that was too worn for school. She was barefoot, and she had Nellie in one arm, pressed tightly against her ribs. Martha noticed her for the first time.

"Have mercy, what's come over you children?" she puzzled. "First you, with your toy truck—"

"Model truck."

"—and now Maggie with her old doll she hasn't played with in years. What in the world? Maggie, you come help, too."

"Help what?" the girl said woodenly.

"Shell these here peas for supper."

"Maggie and I got plans already," her brother said peremptorily, hoping for a quick escape. He took a step down from the porch.

"Hold on there a minute," his mother's voice arrested them. "Maggie's got to help with the shellin' before she goes anywhere."

Jackson turned back. "Why?" he demanded.

Martha gave him a stern look. "Because," she said evenly, "Maggie laid up in the bed this morning and didn't help with lunch, and has done nothing all day but mope. And because I said so, which is reason enough all by itself."

Martha stood, unfolded an aluminum yard chair, and pointed Maggie to it. The girl sat down without protest and took the peas and bowl that were handed to her.

Jackson came back up on the porch with an audibly annoyed sigh.

"Jackson, if these plans of yours are such a matter of life and death," his mother said, "you may go ahead. You've done finished your chores."

"But I promised Maggie I'd take her down to the creek."

"Next time find out what you can or can't do, before you go making promises," Martha advised the boy in a tone of complete indifference.

Jackson flopped down on the old mattress which lay in the corner of the porch. He sulked, "I'm not going without Maggie."

"Suit yourself," Martha murmured.

Maggie popped open one of the pods and slid the purple peas into the small bowl which she had positioned, somewhat precariously, between her knees. The whole process was a little unmanageable, because she wouldn't put Nellie down.

Her mother glanced sideways at her, shook her head mildly, and said nothing.

Mae emptied the meager contents of her bowl into Martha's larger one.

Ever since the stroke, her hands shook so badly that she couldn't accomplish much. Her work on the peas progressed even more slowly than Maggie's. But she was immensely pleased over the opportunity to be useful.

Nathan sat up. He eyed Mae for a moment. "Sonny lets me blow the horn in his big truck," he announced importantly.

Mae smiled.

"He's gonna let me drive it, soon as my feet can reach the pedals," the child went on.

From his corner of the porch Jackson snorted, "Sure he is."

"Jackson," Mama quietly warned.

Nathan lay down on his back and drove the plastic truck across his stomach, motor roaring.

Martha reached down and tapped him on the shoulder. "That'll do."

"I can't play?" the boy protested.

"Yes, if you can do it without all that noise."

"I have to make noise. I'm a truck."

"You won't be a truck much longer if you don't mind," Martha informed him. Then, "Maggie, you could work better if you put that doll down somewhere."

Maggie appeared not to hear.

"You'd get done sooner," Mama pointed out. But she didn't push any further.

Mae looked at Maggie and Nellie with smiling eyes. Little girls and boys shouldn't grow up too fast, she thought. She raised her eyes to Martha's face, wondering if she realized how quickly the years would fly by. With Sonny fully grown, she must have noticed. But then again, with so many younger ones coming along, perhaps she had been too preoccupied.

A pleasant breeze coursed through the sagging screens of the porch, bearing a sweet fragrance from the lily-of-the-valley growing in the woods.

Maggie lifted her face to the breeze. The moving air stirred the delicate, loose strands of her uncombed hair and tickled her face. Maggie knew the place in the woods where the drooping stalks of tiny white bells grew. In her mind she could see the sweet, shy flowers hiding under their shelter of broad green leaves.

Mae also paused in her work, and allowed her trembling hands to rest against the bowl in her lap. She closed her eyes to better catch the scent of the flowers, with its long-past memories from her childhood in this place.

Mae was roused from her memories sometime later by the renewed buzzing noises of Nathan's toy truck.

She opened her eyes and found herself alone with the little boy on the back porch.

From the kitchen came the smell of field peas already cooking.

"Did you have a good nap, Grandma?" Martha asked, coming back out onto the porch.

Mae confessed with a nod, embarrassed. She picked up her small bowl of field peas, and gave it a gentle shake. The handful of peas rattled loosely in the bottom.

She handed the bowl to Martha, shaking her head apologetically.

"We've done fine," Martha said, laying a reassuring hand on her shoulder. "Thank you for helping. Together we've finished them all."

The older woman simply smiled.

"We'll have field peas and snaps for supper tonight, along with chicken and biscuits. Sound good?"

Mae nodded.

Mama's eye fell on Nellie, sitting propped up alone in the lawn chair. She picked the doll up, straightened its dress, and smoothed its hair.

"Nathan," she said, "Where's your sister and brother?"

The little boy stopped scooting across the porch floor on his knees, and sat up to shrug. "Iris got home. Maggie went upstairs. I don't know."

Mama frowned. She glanced toward the edge of the forest, in the direction Jackson had been set on going earlier.

"Those children are up to something," she said decidedly, placing Nellie back in the chair. "But I surely don't knows what."

Lester sat on the front porch steps that afternoon, using his pocketknife to pick dried mud out of the tread of his work shoes. It was slow work, but he was in no hurry. The deepening afternoon shade offered only a little relief from the heat after a hard day in the orchards. He'd had to thin and prune all day. His shoulders ached, but he was proud of the work he'd done. Couldn't begin to count how many trees he tended. Boss even gave him two dollars and a half extra for the day—a bonus—and let him go on home early.

He jabbed a clump of red mud loose, kicked it away from the step, and paused, looking again at the small, blinking kitten half-hidden under Martha's blue hydrangea bush.

"Whur'd you come from?" Lester muttered in an undertone. "I bet I know. Them folks down the road set you out, didn't they? But you needn't plan on settlin' here. Already got more'n we can keep well-fed, as it is."

The kitten looked at him, seeming to listen. She blinked her tiny protruding eyes a few times.

"Yeah, I can see you're a right cute little critter," Les admitted ruefully. "That don't change what is, though."

Jackson came out, letting the screen door bang shut behind him.

"Can't you come out of that door without—" Lester began.

"Sorry, Daddy. I forgot." The boy handed a large glass of iced tea to his father. "Mama told me to bring you this," he explained.

Lester took it with an appreciative nod. "This here was the hottest day we've had on the job since last summer. Thankfully, the sun'll be goin' down soon."

He took several hefty gulps of the iced tea.

"You want some?" Lester offered, raising the glass in his direction. "Cool you down."

Jackson shook his head.

"Your Mama makes the best iced tea," Lester ruminated. "Always has."

Jackson nodded—amiably, he hoped.

Lester looked away from him. The skinny kitten under the hydrangea caught his eye again.

"Son, you see that little cat over yonder—under the flower bush there?"

Jackson hesitated. He said nothing.

Lester's keen eyes searched the boy's face. "I asked you, do you see that cat?" he repeated.

Unwillingly Jackson answered, "Yes, sir."

"I want you to take it somewheres away from here. Take it down to the lake, if you have to. We can't have that thing around here. Maggie sees that little cat, she'll lay claim to it in a skinny minute."

Jackson spoke carefully, after prolonged hesitation. "Daddy—Maggie already knows about the cat."

Lester groaned. He picked up his heavy shoe and began picking at the sole of it again with his knife.

"It might be a good thing," Jackson said cautiously. "Having a cat around. It'll keep away the mice and rats and all."

Lester gave the undersized kitten a sideways glance and answered with a skeptical grunt.

"I'd like to get my hands on whoever put that rascal out on my property! I'm bettin' it was them Jenkins kids. Bet Ralph told 'em to drown the critter, and they hadn't the gumption to do it."

Lester set down the left shoe and began on the right one.

Jackson looked down at his father's feet, long and bony underneath the worn grey socks. He stole a glance at his father's face.

Lester, simultaneously, cast a studying look at his son. Their eyes met.

Jackson pressed his bruised lips together determinedly.

"Daddy, you may as well know right now—there is no way I'm gonna drown Maggie's kitten. I won't do it."

"Maggie's kitten?" Lester echoed.

"Yes, sir."

Lester shut his eyes and shook his head, with a pained expression. He let the shoe drop to the ground. "Maggie done laid claim to that cat, for real?"

Jackson nodded. "Named it and everything."

They both turned their eyes to the shivering ball of fur huddled under the shrub. The kitten looked away, blinked, looked back at them, and looked away again, as if she had understood the meaning of all their conversation.

A mildly warm breeze swept over them. It rustled the oak leaves pleasantly. Lester turned his face to the soft wind, looking out across the fallow acreage south of his house. He took another swallow of tea and handed the glass to Jackson. He picked up the shoe again, scraped as much of the mud off as he was able, and set it side by side with the other one. Then he stretched his aching shoulders and leaned back against the porch post with a long, audible sigh.

Jackson waited for his father to say something. He had already made up his mind, at all cost, to argue for keeping the cat.

But Lester was quiet for a long moment, thinking. Finally, pensively, he spoke. "I reckon a cat that's got itself a name already might as well have a dish of milk or something, round this time of day. It'll sleep better with a full belly."

Jackson's eyes flashed to his father's face. Lester was still gazing out over the dry, stubble field.

"Yes, sir," Jackson said. "I'll see to it right now."

Jackson disappeared inside the house. When he came out again, he had a small plastic dish in his hand, and Maggie beside him, pulling on his arm so excitedly that most of the milk had sloshed out.

They coaxed the kitten out from her shelter. She was very small, and knew no better than to try to drink the milk through her nose. She dipped and sneezed and dipped and sneezed again.

Lester smiled in spite of himself.

"Look," Maggie instructed the kitten, crouching on all fours in front of the dish. "Like this."

"Maggie Burnett, don't you put your face in that dish," came her father's voice.

She sat up quickly, and tried another idea. "Here, kitty," she coaxed, holding out the tip of her finger, dripping with milk.

The kitten's rough tongue caught a drop of milk and searched for more. Maggie put her hand in the dish again, with a hesitant glance at her father.

He nodded. "Just keep your fingers away from your face. Kitten's got worms."

"Worms?"

"That's right."

"Not Percy."

"Percy—??" Lester's eyes widened. He shook his head.

"Daddy's right," Jackson put in. "All kittens do. It's not their fault. Just wash up after you play with her."

Maggie nodded. "Come on. Let's take her up to my room."

"Maybe Iris don't want a cat in her room. Does she know anything about this?" Lester asked, raising an eyebrow.

"I'm gonna go show her now," Maggie replied happily, carrying the kitten snugly against her chest. "Come on," she said to Jackson.

The children darted inside the front door, mumbling quick apologies to Martha, who was bumped off balance on her way out.

"Well—!" she caught her breath, folding her skirt under her and sitting down beside her husband on the porch step. "I guess the kitten's staying?"

"I reckon so," he grumbled.

Martha laid her head against Lester's shoulder. The cool of the coming evening, after the heat of day, made her feel drowsy and contented.

"How in the world did she come up with Percy for a name?" Lester growled after a minute. "Percy ain't no kind of name for a cat. Girl cat, to boot."

Martha sighed, "Who knows what goes on in that child's head."

"We don't need a cat," Lester pointed out. "Percy or any other fool name."

"No. We don't," she agreed.

They were both silent for a few minutes. Lester's arm slid around his wife's waist.

She glanced into his eyes and away again. Softly, she murmured against his shoulder, "But Les, did you see how it made that young'uns face light up?"

Lester nodded. "I saw."

"You did a good thing, saying yes."

A small, sad smile softened Lester's dark eyes and tanned countenance.

"I was too hard on the child yesterday. Her teacher had got me so riled up, Martha. But I know how it is with Maggie. I ought to have known. I mean—she's different from our other children. Maybe she's a little— what is it they call it now? —slow. Ain't her fault if it's that. She's how God made her."

Martha laid her head on his shoulder, in agreement. "I'm real glad to hear you say that, Les."

Lester ruminated about his younger daughter. "Teacher said she don't try in school. Then she said she can't get Maggie's attention." He paused. "Martha, that don't sound to me like the same thing, exactly."

"I don't know, honey."

"Teacher said some other things I didn't understand. Something about—I don't know—Maggie not spelling things right. She had some fancy name for it. Well, hun, I never won no spelling bee, myself—did you?"

Martha shook her head against his shoulder, her thoughts wandering. It was nice to be close to Lester like this, just listening to him talk. He was almost never home this early in the day.

"Well, I tell you what. More I think on it, I believe Jackson may have been right. Maggie's teacher don't much like her."

"For a fact?" Martha roused slightly.

"Well, I can't say for a fact. But there was things she *didn't* say. Important things, like how Maggie—well, you know. She's got a sweetness to her. Different from Iris. Oh, Iris is a fine girl, but she's awful smart, coming home with her marks all A's. And a smart teenager can get right sneaky."

"I wouldn't know," Martha said, smiling wryly at her husband.

He grinned and tightened his arm around her shoulder, squeezing her close to him.

"Girl, you are bright and sweet, too—and pretty as a speckled pup," he declared.

"Listen to yourself talkin' foolishness," she murmured, leaning in to him.

He held her closer. His voice fell low. "Martha, what's wrong with me? How come—" the words eluded him. He began again, with his wife's curious gaze on his face. "You don't lose *your* temper with the kids."

"Only every single day," she confessed with a small smile.

He looked in her eyes, puzzled. "Well, you don't show it."

"Oh—sometimes I do."

He sighed. "I'm feelin' real bad about punching Jackson. I'm not sure what I should've done, but not that. He's got a scab on his lip now. And a black eye." Lester's brow furrowed.

Martha met his eyes, listening.

Lester was disturbed, angry about it, as if someone else had caused it. "Why the devil does he have a black eye?" he fretted. "I didn't hit him in the eye. I know I didn't. I shouldn't have hit him at all," he concluded miserably.

"Your temper gets away with you sometimes, Les," his wife agreed mildly. "Don't be too hard on yourself. You're only raising your children the same way you were raised. Your daddy was a hard man, I remember."

"Mm," Lester assented, his mind refusing to leave his earlier question.

"But why is his eye all purple underneath? I swear I didn't hit his eye, Martha."

"He had a nosebleed; sometimes the bruising from that will spread upwards. And all around. Martha looked sorrowfully at her husband, who sat now with his arms folded over his knees, his head bent down so low that his forehead was touching the back of his wrist. She had been upset with him for the very reason she now sought to comfort him. It occurred to her that life was strange that way. How it seemed to curl back on itself like a vine sometimes. And oh, the tangles it could wrap itself into.

"Lester, you dearly love your children. I know you do."

He nodded miserably, not raising his head.

"They know it, too."

To this there was no response. With a sigh, Martha laid her hand on her husband's shoulders and rubbed the taut, knotted muscles.

It was around four-thirty when Martha went in to begin supper and Lester climbed the stairs for a nap.

She put several cups of flour into a mixing bowl, added buttermilk, salt, and a large spoonful of Crisco. She began kneading rhythmically.

Mae was lying down, too, as she did some part of every afternoon. From her room came soft murmurs of Maggie talking to her new kitten. Martha smiled to herself. She had not heard so many words from Maggie since—she couldn't think when. Maggie and Iris had taken to Mae, that was for sure. The boys did not take much notice of her. But they hadn't complained.

Truthfully, Mae had not been a burden, as Martha had feared. She was just a gentle old soul who helped in the kitchen when she could, stayed in her room most of the day, and didn't complain.

Her flow of thoughts and the easy silence were both broken by the sound of her son's voice.

"Mama—?" Jackson said in a guarded tone. "Can you come here a minute? Please?"

Martha was up to her elbows in Gold Bond white flour, rolling out dough for the biscuits. "Jackson—" she said, startled. "Can't you see I'm —"

She looked up and was surprised to see Iris standing in the kitchen doorway beside him.

"What is it—" Martha said in a flat quick voice, filled with sudden dread. "What's happened, what's wrong?"

Iris came into the kitchen and took her mother by the arm.

"Nothing's wrong, Mama. Come in the living room."

Martha wiped her hands and arms, left her baking, and allowed Iris to lead her into the living room.

The room was empty, except for the sofa and chair, floor lamp and cabinet. Nothing was in any way changed. She looked from one to the other of her children, silently demanding an explanation.

Then the screen door faintly creaked.

A thin young man wearing a grey plaid shirt and worn grey trousers stepped across the threshold. He stopped just inside the door. He waited, his gaze penetratingly fixed on the floor, unwilling to come further into the house.

Martha stared, silent and motionless as death. All the color drained from her face. She looked dazedly from Iris to Jackson to the newcomer. Then she closed her eyes for a long moment. When she opened them again, they were flooded with tears. Silently the tears spilled over.

Iris and Jackson exchanged an anxious glance.

Loosening her arm from Iris's grasp, Martha slowly crossed the room, quietly bridging the distance between herself and her long-absent son. Her cheeks were flushed pink with color now. And although she did not smile, her hands were infinitely tender as she wrapped her arms around his shoulders. She laid her head down against his neck as if she had found her final, long-awaited place of rest.

Reuben's hands came up slowly, hesitantly; his rough palms gently pressed against her shoulder blades, returning her embrace.

"Mama," he whispered so softly that only a mother could hear.

Lester slept through until supper time. When he came downstairs, smoothing down his pillow-skewed hair, he sensed something different and alien in the quietness that greeted him. His footsteps slowed suspiciously. As he turned the landing, he could see all of his family standing at the dinner table, waiting for him. But there was no talking, no chatter. It was like a military formation. Then he saw the reason. He stopped in his tracks. He cast accusing eyes at Sonny, who answered with a slight shake of his head: don't look at me, it wasn't my doing.

Next he looked to Martha, but her eyes were averted. The other children were watching him anxiously; except for Reuben, who's eyes were turned intently downward, staring through the place setting directly in front of him, without seeing it.

Lester simply stood on the third step for a moment. The tension in the room was as thick as the pot roast Martha had prepared. Lester's narrowed eyes indicated disapproval, but he did not speak.

He looked intently at each face around the table. The children were eager to accept their long-missing brother. Their young faces were open books. Powerfully ambivalent feelings stirred within him. His temper flared, then cooled. All of his children were here, together. And his wife, looking younger than she had this morning; and his grandmother, hands trembling, as always, on the rim of her chair. More family than he had ever had together at one time before. All eyes, with the exception of Reuben's, were fixed on him, in mingled apprehension and hope.

Reuben, in silence, kept his eyes on the edge of the table, gazing at nothing, waiting.

Everyone and everything waited—as if time itself held its breath—to see what Lester would say.

He clumped down the remaining stairs, his face hard and set. He took his seat at the head of the table, as if nothing were out of the ordinary. But his hostile face betrayed him.

No one moved.

"What are you waiting for, Martha?" Les demanded. "Serve up the food."

Quickly she began to dish food onto plates from the pots on the stove, passing them around. Several bowls were already filled and set on the table within easy reach.

"Looks good, Mama," Sonny ventured, unnerved by the cold silence.

"Thank you, son." She turned to the stove and piled mashed potatoes onto her oldest son's plate. When she turned to hand it to him, she saw with a pang that Reuben had left his seat without a sound and was nowhere to be seen. She hesitated. In the four long years of his absence, never had his chair looked so empty. She let the serving spoon fall into the gravy and half-turned, thinking to seek him out.

"Tend to dinner," Lester instructed her, guessing her intent. Reluctantly she did as he said. With all plates served, the family bowed their heads for the blessing.

There was a brief, awkward silence.

"Martha." Lester spoke the word with severity.

With mingled sorrow and quiet dignity, Martha murmured, "Lord, bless this food to our use and us to Thy service. Amen."

Sonny spoke up nervously. "Pass the biscuits this here way, Maggie, while they're still hot."

Jackson cast a glance across the table to Iris. There was concern in his eyes. Iris answered with a grim expression.

"Clingstone peaches are coming in thick," Lester informed the gathered group. "Gonna be a long day at work tomorrow, I'm thinking."

No one dared reply.

No further conversation was attempted. Supper was finished in uneasy silence.

The first minute she could get away, Martha located Reuben sitting in the darkness of the back porch steps. "Honey, I saved you some supper," she began. "Ever'body else is done."

"He don't want me here, Mama." Reuben controlled his voice carefully, but his mother could tell he had been crying.

Softly she sat down beside him on the sturdiest of the rotting steps.

"Yes he does. He just don't know it yet." She laid her arm gently around Reuben's shoulder.

"Don't know if this step will hold the both of us," he cautioned her, with a quirk of a smile, faintly visible by moonlight. "Daddy hasn't done much to keep the place up, has he?"

"Don't have the time. Or money," Martha replied simply.

"Mama," Reuben began, then fell into an unexplained silence.

"I'm listening," she prompted him, craning her neck, trying to see his face.

He cleared his throat. "If Daddy don't run me off afore I can do it, I'll fix these steps for you. And anything else you want done. I learned a lot of skills in—the—where I was. I can fix near about anything."

"That'd be wonderful, Reuben. I'd be so glad." She gave his shoulder a squeeze. "I know you must be tired, son. I'm going to make up a bed for you in the spare room. There's a cot. It's not the Holiday Inn, but—it's home."

The boy closed weary eyes. "That's all I want in this world, Mama."

Her throat closed up, making her unable to speak. She kissed his cheek and stood, leaving to go prepare his room.

While Martha put fresh sheets on the cot in the spare room for Reuben, Lester watched the boy's silhouette, silently, from a corner of the porch completely engulfed in shadow. He had heard the conversation between Martha and their son. He pondered what he could say to the boy. What would be the right choice to make.

Martha prepared a tray, bearing two cups of coffee. She had hoped for further time with Reuben, now that the younger children were settled for the night. But as she turned toward the back porch, Lester stepped into the kitchen.

"Have him to meet me on the front porch," Lester told her. "We'll talk. You don't need to come. He can bring the tray."

Martha simply nodded.

The stars were out in countless numbers—a vast display. Stars were less visible in the city because of the many electric lights. Constellations seldom if ever seen in prison.

Reuben brought the coffee and handed one mug to his father in silence. He stood on the front porch, his eyes fixed on the sky, painfully homesick for his lost youth in the beautiful countryside of the upstate. In the distance, a glow of pale warm light on the horizon identified the city of Spartanburg.

The screen door creaked and then was quietly shut. Lester looked around to see what the interruption was. It was merely Martha, silently placing a plate of cookies on the porch table.

"Sit down, boy," Lester instructed, pointing to the steps below him. He was sitting on the top step, leaning against the porch post. Reuben, interpreting this as an indication of rank, a reminder of his damaged position in the family hierarchy, took his seat two steps below his father.

Lester sipped at the almost scalding coffee and made a face, unseen in the dark. What wouldn't he give for a cigarette tonight? But this conversation would be nothing like the one with Sonny. He was infinitely uncomfortable in the presence of this son.

Minutes ticked by. Reuben said nothing, and neither did his father. It began to look as though they would finish their coffee, and most of the cookies, and retire without ever speaking. But finally Lester broke the silence.

"So how you been, son?" he asked Reuben in a slightly awkward attempt to be less threatening.

Reuben slowly shook his head.

"That don't tell me much of nothin'," his father said with a wan smile.

Reuben looked down at his hands cupping the coffee mug. He sighed deeply. He spoke quietly, and with effort.

"I'm beat up, Daddy. Just about to death. Twenty-four years old and done already tore up my chances at having any kind of a life. Now here I am sitting on your porch step, not knowing if you're even going to let me stay the night."

Lester was unprepared for this brief burst of honesty.

"Your Mama's made up the cot in the upstairs room," he answered in a smooth, toneless voice. "You can stay the night."

He heard the boy's sigh of relief and murmured thanks.

"You *could* have eat supper with us," Lester said reprovingly. "'Stead of running off hiding on the back porch steps."

"I didn't know. I wasn't sure. I—I was afraid I'd be imposing." Reuben didn't add that he had hoped for a fragment of welcome. The simple sound of his name spoken. An acknowledgment. Anything. He would have stayed and eaten with the family.

"You talked to Sonny since you been back?" his father wanted to know.

Reuben shook his head, not looking up.

"Sonny gave me your message. Asking if you could come home." Lester paused. "I told him no."

Reuben hung his head. "I swear I didn't know."

"I believe you. Anyways, you're here now. That changes some things. For one, your mother is counting heavy on gettin' to keep you. And the children are right curious about all what's goin' on."

"I'll leave in the morning, before you all get up," Reuben offered. " I'll just disappear."

Lester chuckled. "You'd have a right big task to get up earlier in the morning than your mama and I do."

"I'll tell Mama I can't stay. That I never planned on staying, just stopped by to see her. I won't let the blame go to you. It don't belong to you."

Lester's brow furrowed. This was a different Reuben than the rebellious boy he'd so disturbingly remembered. But Lester wasn't born yesterday. This could all be for show. His boy could be playing him.

"I believe we need to talk over some things, son. Before you think about leaving or staying."

Reuben was silent.

"Can't we have a decent conversation like two grown men?" his father pressed.

"These steps need work," Reuben noted, distracted by the give in the board beneath his feet.

"You think I don't know that?" Lester retorted, taking offense. "You think I'm blind or something? When in the world would I have time to fix 'em? I work morning to night, for crying out loud."

"I didn't mean nothing," Reuben said, shamed. "I—I just was gonna say that I'd fix them for you. I learned a lot about—woodworking—" his voice trailed off.

"Oh." Lester drank his coffee, which had mellowed to a proper warmth. He passionately longed for a cigarette. He drew a deep sigh, and plunged in to what he wanted to communicate.

"You know why life is so hard, son?"

Reuben raised weary eyes obediently to his father's face.

"Life is hard when people care enough to do what's right. When people work, and take responsibility. Do the right thing. That's what makes life hard, but it's also what makes it worth living. That's what you've got yet to learn."

Reuben shook his head slightly. "I don't know, Daddy. I think life's just hard any way it comes."

Again Lester frowned. This young man was like a stranger. True, he had been a child of few words. But now, as a man, he was still more reticent—as if words, or even life itself, had somehow become his enemy. For an instant, Lester wanted to wipe the slate clean, welcome the boy with open arms, help him rebuild his strength and courage. But he couldn't just pretend the intervening years had never happened.

He clenched his teeth. Reuben had disdained the straight and narrow path. He had tried to take the easy way. He had shamed the family, and the name of Burnett. This was not something Lester could easily forgive. But the boy was near broken. The father felt it in his heart.

"Tell you what, son." He spoke quietly, reasonably. "Let's give this thing a try." He nodded, as if to encourage himself. "We'll just give it a try, and who knows? Maybe it'll work out."

Reuben looked up into his father's eyes. His lips parted as if to speak, but no words followed. There was just the sadness in his eyes, the ache.

Lester laid a hand on the boy's shoulder. "Come on, son, let's get you settled in. You could use some sleep for sure."

Reuben was up before dawn. He would not rest, it seemed, until Martha appointed him some work to do to help compensate for his room and board.

"The steps, back and front need mending," he told his mother at breakfast.

"We'll have to buy some new wood planks, I guess," she said uncertainly, looking to Lester.

"I'll bring 'em in with me tonight," he promised. "Just give me the measurements you need."

"Reuben, it'll be mighty fine to have those steps new and straight and strong," his mother smiled.

"That's for sure," Sonny echoed. Only the adults had lingered at table.

"What can I do today?" Reuben wanted to know. "Meanwhile?"

"Well, let me give it some thought. If you really want to, you can help me with these dishes, for one thing."

"Sure."

Sonny and Lester left the kitchen, talking about Sonny's latest delivery, while Martha and her younger son cleared the table. She ran hot sudsy water for the dishes.

Glancing around, to be sure the men were gone, she confided to Reuben, "Son, you don't have to work every minute, just relax. Be at home. Do whatever you'd be doing if you'd never gone away."

He shook his head. "That was a life-time ago. I wouldn't know how."

"Well, get some practice. Get to know your brothers and sisters again. And Mae."

"The old lady," Reuben recalled. "I been meaning to ask you about her. Who is she, where'd she come from? If it's okay for me to ask," he added hastily.

Martha actually laughed, half-turning to look at him without dripping dishwater on the floor. "Nobody's told you—? I guess not. I thought maybe you and your dad would have talked about it last night."

"We didn't talk a whole lot."

"Oh." Martha waited in case her son might say more. But he didn't.

"Well," she answered, turning back to the sink, " Mae is your daddy's grandma—we do not call her 'the old lady' by the way," she noted quietly. "Grandma grew up in this house, and she came to live with us just lately. She's a right sweet little thing. She hasn't been any trouble to speak of."

"Daddy's grandma?" Reuben looked puzzled. "I don't remember ever seeing her before."

"Once or twice, when you were real small. She didn't live around here. 'Course, she looked different then, and—anyway I wouldn't expect you to remember. You want to give me a hand with these dishes, son? Right there's a clean towel to dry them with."

He was quick to respond, apologetic for letting his attention wander. A small pain throbbed in Martha's throat, and she wished she had not asked him to help. He was too obedient, too eager to please her. It didn't feel natural. All of her children were obedient, but each had his or her own way of mildly protesting. Nathan whined. Iris made excuses. *And* whined. Jackson was pretty good about helping, but sometimes he balked. Sonny inevitably had other plans that somehow popped up on the spur of the moment. And Maggie simply forget what she started out to do.

"You really ought to get to know the children better," Martha said with a wry smile. "They're every one of 'em a piece of work. Can't help but love 'em, all the same."

Reuben smiled slightly, focused on drying dishes, and wondering what he could do after that.

"I think I'll chop some firewood, Mama."

"Honey, it's springtime! We got the whole summer and fall ahead of us."

"I know, but this way I can put some in the shed to start drying out. And—I may not—" he bit his tongue before saying what was in his mind. Smoothly he altered the words. "I may not have time, if Daddy puts me on a big project, like maybe painting the house. There's a lot of work needing to be done, Mama."

"Don't I know," she sighed.

"I can do every bit of it," he pledged. "I've learned the skills. I just need materials. And they cost money. Which—I—don't have." His voice trailed off. He had talked himself into an embarrassing corner. He felt his face flush hot.

"We'll take it one thing at a time," Mama said easily, sensing his shame, and moving the conversation quickly in a new direction. "Oh, listen, have you seen Jackson's drawings? I want you to be sure to look at them. He's a regular artist, turns out." She paused. Reuben made no comment. "He won a blue ribbon at school for a big poster he drew of a Civil War battle," she prompted.

"That so?" the boy finally said, preoccupied with drying flatware.

She hesitated. Reuben had never been one to keep up a conversation. But this new reticence was unpredictable. He seemed to drop in and out. Like a turtle, venturing only a tiny bit out of his shell, then closing up tightly at any uncertainty. She wondered what experiences he had known in the years they had been apart, to make him this way. The question burdened her, but she knew better than to ask.

She shook off these sad thoughts as she shook her hands free of the greasy grey dishwater.

"All done!" she announced, smiling at Reuben. "Thank you, son."

"Yes, ma'am. You're more'n welcome. I'll go chop some firewood."

"Seriously, we won't need firewood for months yet."

"Well, I want to get started on it. Can't hurt to have it done."

He left her, then, without another word. Through the window she watched him stride across the back yard to the logs piled at the edge of the woods. She carefully denied a nagging fear that he might not be planning to still be home by winter.

The axe was imbedded in a big oak stump. He pried it loose, heaved a thick log to stand vertically on top of the stump, and with careful aim split it in two.

Martha shook her head sadly. "That boy is troubled in his soul. Lord help him."

Reuben didn't stop splitting logs for forty-five minutes. Then he paused, breathing heavily, letting his arm muscles have a moment to relax.

Martha, who had been checking on him through the window from time to time, called to Maggie.

The little girl was lying on her stomach in the living room floor, lining up dominoes and stacking them in varying patterns. The kitten napped in a sunbeam from the window. When Martha came into the room, she inadvertently bumped one of the small stacks of dominoes with her shoe.

"Oh—!" Maggie jumped to her feet, looked wildly at her mother, and dropped to the floor again, hastily restoring the little rectangular blocks to their former position. Her face had crumpled, and she was trying to hold back tears.

"Maggie," her mother said in a soft voice. "I didn't mean to mess up your play. I'm sorry."

The girl looked up at her and the brimming tears ran down.

"Oh, Maggie...." Martha knelt in the floor and put her arms around the distraught child. "Maggie, Maggie. What *does* go on in your mind?"

She reached out to help replace the dominoes, but the child quickly broke loose from her embrace, and with careful gentleness pushed her mother's hand aside, explaining, "No, I have to do it."

Martha waited patiently as the little one corrected her pattern and slowly calmed herself.

"All better?" her mother asked tentatively.

Maggie nodded.

"Do you think you can do something for Mama?"

Another nod.

"Your brother Reuben is working out in the hot sun. Could you take him a glass of water for me, and wait while he drinks it, and bring the glass back in?"

Maggie looked ruefully at her domino domain. "Where's Nathan?"

"I'm not sure I can trust him with a heavy glass quite yet."

"But—I mean, will he mess up my dominoes while I'm gone?"

"No. He's busy with his own doin's upstairs."

"He might come down," Maggie pointed out, lip quivering.

"I'll make sure everything is safe," Mama promised. "Come along," she encouraged, going back to the kitchen. She filled a large glass with water and ice. "He'll be real glad to get this," she said, handing it to Maggie with care. "Got hold of it, there? Good girl."

Maggie carried the water slowly and carefully across the yard. When she reached Reuben, she transferred the glass safely into his hands.

"Thanks," he acknowledged. "Maggie-Muffin, right? That's what Iris calls you?"

"She calls me Raggymuffin, mostly," the child corrected.

"Oh."

Reuben sat down on one of the cinder blocks which happened to be lying purposelessly to one side. Maggie waited, as instructed, to bring the glass back to the kitchen.

But Reuben took his time. He was hot and the drink was too cold to take all at once. He sipped at it and looked around him, past the dirt yard to the lush, green woods beyond. He looked everywhere except at Maggie.

"I heard about Jackson shooting a snake down yonder," he remarked after a minute.

Maggie didn't answer.

Her brother gave her a half-glance. "Must've been some snake."

Maggie said, "Daddy hit him."

Reuben was momentarily confused. "Sonny told me wrong, then. He said it was Jackson that killed it."

"No, I mean—Daddy hit Jackson," the girl explained.

"Oh."

"'Cause he took Daddy's gun. Daddy hit his mouth and—" Maggie paused, suddenly self-conscious at her own verbosity "—there was—a lot of blood," she finished quickly, and fell silent.

Reuben nodded slightly.

The kitten, Percy, had been hiding out in the top branches of the oak tree while all the chopping was going on below. With the noise stopped, and the sound of her mistress's voice, she came scrambling awkwardly down, now—half-climbing, half-falling. She landed, mostly by chance, on all four feet with a soundless thump. For a moment, she just stood there, stunned, blinking her eyes.

Reuben looked at her with an expression that was very nearly a smile.

"C'mere, you," he said softly, holding out his hand to the kitten. "Come on, now."

To Maggie's surprise, her kitten responded.

Reuben set down the glass of ice water and picked Percy up, scratching behind her ears in a friendly way. The kitten settled in his lap without hesitation, purring.

Maggie looked anxiously up into her brother's dark face.

Reaching for his drink, he caught the look with a glance, and instantly understood it.

"Everybody's told you to be careful of me, haven't they? They've told you I'm bad, I reckon?" Reuben said, a little defensively.

Maggie nodded meekly.

Her honesty disarmed him. He stroked the kitten thoughtfully for a minute. "It's true I guess," he said with reluctance. "But there's different kinds of bad. I wouldn't hurt your kitten for nothin'—you needn't worry about that."

Maggie lowered her eyes. She did not know what to say.

"How'd you get your daddy to let you have a cat, anyhow?" Reuben asked, changing the subject.

"Jackson talked him into it," she answered, barely above a whisper.

"Jackson," Reuben repeated, with that same half-smile. "He's a piece of work, now, ain't he?"

He handed the kitten to Maggie, finished his water in one gulp, and stood to resume his labor.

"Jackson's near a man, now," he remarked. "I didn't recognize him when he showed up at—when I first saw him again. Iris has grown up, too. And you. You don't remember me, probably. Nathan was a baby, just getting his sea legs—" Reuben hesitated. He was not used to conversation of this nature. The sound of his own voice made him suddenly uncomfortable.

He dumped out the ice and handed the empty glass back to Maggie. "I got to work now," he told her, shortly. "You need to get outa the way." He motioned with his hand.

She backed up a few steps.

"Go on," he directed. "Go on back in the house." She wandered a few reluctant steps in that direction.

Reuben picked up the axe, swung it easily, and split a fresh log perfectly in two. He had learned and honed the skills of manual labor during his time in prison. He hoisted one of the halves upright on the stump and was poised to split it when he was arrested by his sister's small voice.

"Are you home to stay?" she wanted to know.

Reuben lowered the axe and straightened his shoulders, not looking directly at her. He thought he detected a tentative hope in her voice. He drew a deep sigh, staring back out over the green woods.

"For a while," he answered. "I don't know how long." He dared not look at her face. "I got to work now, hear? Get away, so's you don't get hurt. I mean it. Git." He watched until Maggie was fully inside the house. Then he split the half-log with a single, well-aimed stroke.

When Reuben finally looked up from stacking the split logs neatly between two tree trunks, he was drenched in sweat. The sweat ran off his lengthy bangs and into his eyes, partially blinding him. For an instant, between that and the sun glaring in his line of vision, he did not recognize the figure standing a mere five or six feet away. He frowned. "Sonny?" he questioned tentatively, rubbing the sweat out of his blurred eyes.

He heard an all-too-familiar sneer. "You been chopping and stacking too much wood, my friend. Workin' too hard. Got you addled, I'm thinkin'."

It seemed to Reuben that his blood ran ice cold beneath his over-heated exterior.

"You." He spoke the word without emotion. "How the devil did you find me here?"

"You weren't at the cabin. So I prowled around a bit. I got my ways. That's a fact you might want to tuck away for future reference." He smiled wickedly.

"I told you never to come anywhere near my house or my family," Reuben reminded him, seething.

"Well—*delighted* to see you, too, good buddy," the young man known as Bo said with a sarcastic half-smile. "Oh, I thought—bein' as I hadn't heard from you —maybe I'd better stop by and remind you of our deal."

Reuben picked up another quarter log and heaved it onto the top of the shoulder-high pile. His jaw was clenched tightly, as if to prevent any further conversation.

"Oh, now," Bo murmured smoothly, "you can't have forgotten our deal, can you?"

Reuben ignored him, continuing to stack wood, although he was growing dizzy and his heart was pounding.

"See here, Rube, you still owe Kobra a lot of money. You owe me some, too, while we're at it. How you planning to make good on that? If you don't pay Kobe off in a reasonable period of time, well—there's consequences." He explained pointedly with a sickening grin. "What can I say? Sometimes people get hurt."

Reuben straightened. His head was buzzing. He faced his former friend squarely.

"What do you want, Bo? What'd you come here for? Say it quick and be on your way."

Bo grinned outright. "Why, I swear if that don't sound downright unfriendly somehow. But, being as that's the way you feel, I'll get down to business. Kobra's getting all of us together. Everybody. Got a time and a place set. He's got us a sure-fire job lined up. See, he owes Hank. Everybody owes somebody, I reckon. We'll make a small fortune on this bank job. Then we're going to cross over to North Carolina and get our money that's stashed there. Then Virginia. After that we can split if we want to and lay low 'til the smoke settles."

"Not me. I'm out of it," Reuben said quietly, but with an edge to his voice.

"I don't want my share of the money. I don't want to see Kobra or any of you guys ever again. I've put that behind me. I'm making a new start."

Bo chuckled. It was a sinister sound that sent cold chills up Reuben's spine.

"You don't really think you can do that? Just start over?" Bo stated, disbelieving. "You gotta be even dumber than I ever gave you credit for."

"Get lost," Reuben returned flatly.

"Hey. You got to tie up loose ends, my friend. Then—after that—you'll have options."

Reuben looked his comrade straight in the eye. His nostrils flared with suppressed anger. "What is it you want, Bo? What do you want me to say that'll make you leave?"

"I just want your word that you'll meet me this time next week at sundown. You know where. We'll finalize our plans then. You got to follow through this last round, man. You got a downright supernatural skill for pickin' a lock or crackin' a safe. Smooth as silk. Never seen the like. Just one more job—then you can try starting a new life if you still want to. We're all going separate ways, at least 'til the dust settles."

Reuben saw his mother come into the kitchen. From the kitchen window, he could see the pale sand color of her house dress. Any minute she could lean out to ask him how everything was going.

"By the way," Bo inquired smoothly. "Who was that little cupcake you were talking to just now? Pretty little thing. That your kid sister?"

Reuben found his voice. "Naw, Just some neighbor kid hanging around over here."

Bo tipped his head back with a curiously knowing smile. "Nuh-uh. I don't think so. She looks just like you in the face. You got yourself another sister, too. Older. Real pretty girl. Sure would hate to see anything happen to either one of 'em."

Reuben glanced back at the house, nervously.

"I'll be there, all right?" he said hastily. "But after this, no more. Now go. Get out of here."

"I'm going," Bo said, tipping his black cowboy hat politely. But his smile beneath its circle of shade was dark and cold. "Tuesday week at sundown. And if you start to lose your nerve, just remember your two sisters and what I told—"

Reuben's temper exploded. He swung at Bo and caught him hard on the chin. Bo staggered backwards and fell, scraping his head against the rough and splintery wood of the chopping block. Blood spurted from a rip in the skin above his eyebrow, filling his eye and momentarily blinding him. He peered up at Reuben, squinting through hot blood.

"I can make threats, too," Reuben informed him coldly. He raised the long-handled axe high and brought it down with a shattering blow, embedding it in the stump a careful five inches from Bo's head. "So don't be messin' with me."

Bo forced himself to stand, disoriented though he was. He looked hard at Reuben, both eyes narrowed bitterly, dripping blood from the brow wound. "You'll pay for this," he vowed in a voice choked with rage. "I'll watch you die! I swear I will!" He made his way, stumbling, into the cover of the forest surrounding the house and was finally out of sight.

Reuben's sigh seemed to drain his very soul.

"Reuben?" Martha called out the open window.

Reuben shuddered, dreading to know whether his mother had witnessed the violence. He walked slowly toward the house, hoping to go straight to his room, but his mother's voice, inevitably, intervened.

"I saw you talking with somebody. I was just making lemonade to bring out to the both of you."

Her son's footsteps slowed. Relief flooded him. She hadn't seen everything. The tall young man turned to her, his weight on one leg, face turned down.

"He was in a hurry," Reuben explained. "He had to—be somewhere."

"Oh. Well. Maybe next time. Friend of yours?"

Reuben's jaw tightened. "Just a guy I know."

Martha eyed him with a trace of a frown. "Reuben?"

"I'm sorry about that there, Mama," he said, gesturing vaguely toward the back yard. "Him coming around here. Won't happen again."

Martha's eyes lowered. She carefully modulated her facial expression to show no emotion. "Then he wasn't a friend?"

Reuben shrugged, his gaze fixed on the floor. "We used to be friends." He chewed his lower lip, debating how much to divulge. "He was—serving time same place as me. We were buddies, yeah. For awhile anyhow."

A shadow passed over Martha's face, unseen by Reuben's downcast eyes.

"Are you in trouble, son?" Her voice was lowered, as if she wished to hide the unavoidable question from both of them.

"No, ma'am. No trouble. Nothing for you to worry yourself over." There was a pause. A burdened silence.

"Reuben, are you telling me the truth?" Martha pressed gently.

He couldn't look in her face, though he tried. Still with eyes fixed on the floor he mumbled, "I hope so, Mama."

He turned away then, walked quietly to his room, and shut the door.

The weekend rolled around. That Saturday night, in bed, when Martha asked her husband about going to church in the morning, she only got a groan of misery in reply. She sighed. She understood that Lester was worn out from working all week. Still, he had been missing more Sundays than he had managed to attend. She didn't want her sons getting the idea that church was for the women-folk.

She rolled over in bed. Her eyes were wide open in the dark. She had Reuben on her mind. And the mysterious stranger who had come by to talk to him. She had not told Lester, and this worried her. But she knew Lester would send their son away, at any hint of trouble. She lay awake into the pre-dawn hours.

Nevertheless, she woke early in the morning and rose without a sound. She took her Sunday clothes into the bathroom and dressed there, so she wouldn't waken Lester. She could tell by the way his face was pressed into the pillow, adapting to its shape like a lump of clay, that he had slept hard and would sleep hours more if not disturbed.

Quietly she put on her finest Sunday outfit. She would invite Mae to go with her. Jackson, Maggie and Nathan had no choice. Sonny had left again to make a delivery in Nancy, Kentucky and would be gone a week. Martha didn't much like to drive, but she was able. She would invite Reuben, too, but doubted he would accept. Iris had gotten in late and was as exhausted as her father. However, Maggie's movements, and the whispering around her, awakened the girl.

"How's a person s'posed to get any sleep with y'all buzzing around like a bunch of mosquitoes?" she demanded, raising her head and rubbing her reddened eyes.

"It's time to get up and get ready for church."

"Church?" Iris frowned. "It's Sunday already?"

Martha smiled wryly. "I 'spect you remember last night—Saturday night?"

Iris roused herself fully awake. "I'm getting up, Mama. I'll be ready." She didn't want to miss Grandma's first Sunday at their church.

"You could wear what you had on last night—excepting it's bad wrinkled," Martha said pointedly.

Iris blushed. She hastened into the bathroom to get her shower.

They arrived at the Holston Creek Baptist church just as everyone was making the transition from Sunday School to Worship. There were clusters of people standing on the front lawn, chatting. As one, they turned to look when Martha drove up in the old Buick. There were expressions of surprise as Mae was helped out of the back seat. Preacher Lawson came personally to walk her up the steps to the church and introduce her to everyone along the way.

"Y'all be good," Mama whispered to her children. "I mean, *extra* good, hear?"

A chorus of "Yes, ma'am."

Martha drew a deep breath and straightened her hat—the one with the pink flowers around the band—and taking Maggie and Nathan by the hand, she plunged into the buzzing crowd.

She seated herself and the children quickly, hoping to escape some of the inevitable gossip, and likely queries about Lester's absence. Briskly, she found the hymn numbers in the hymnal and tore off small pieces from the church bulletin to mark their places. She was thankful when the organist began to play, and the preacher settled Mae in the pew beside her and walked up to take his place at the front of the church.

Martha glanced at Mae with a smile. She lightly patted her knee. This was to say she was pleased to have Mae here with them at church. Women understood these small gestures and the magnitude of their meanings.

Mae returned the smile, but her eyes were moist with held-back tears. Martha gave her a quizzical look, but then the first hymn started and everyone stood to sing.

> *Oh, Love that will not let me go,*
> *I rest my weary soul in Thee;*
> *I give Thee back the life I owe,*
> *that in Thine ocean depths its flow*
> *may richer, fuller be. -George Matheson*

By the second verse, the tears were silently streaking down Mae's wrinkled cheeks. Martha nudged her gently out of the pew and out of the church, glad they had chosen seats near the back.

"Grandma, what's wrong?" she asked, putting an arm around the older woman's shoulder. "What made you so sad?"

Mae shook her head dismissively.

"Yes, it is *too* something. You can tell me, Grandma," Martha whispered gently. "Do you want me to get Iris? She knows how to talk to you and what you are saying back."

The large cloudy blue eyes looked Martha full in the face. The voiceless sorrow in them sent a pang through the young mother's heart. She reached and smoothed the white hair back from the troubled brow with a soft touch.

Hesitantly, Mae took Martha by the hand and walked with her outdoors to the side of the church. There was a graveyard there, adorned with headstones, markers, gravel, vases and scraggly plastic flowers. Each grave was framed in a narrow railing of wood two inches high.

Martha took in the scene with instant understanding. "You have people here, don't you, Grandma?"

Together they wove their way forward, stepping around the burial plots, keeping to the pathways in between. Martha saw a large headstone with Burnett engraved on it.

"I've seen this before," she murmured. "I never stopped to think..."

But it was not this that had snagged Mae's heart and brought her to tears.

She pressed on a little further and stopped before a tiny grave devoid of a marker. There was only a small chipped porcelain vase, empty, and a white lamb borrowed from some ancient Nativity set.

Tears sprang up in Martha's eyes, now, too. "This was—?" she questioned as delicately as possible.

Mae nodded, her lips pressed together. She made a sign with her hands, indicating something of small size. She whispered a monosyllable, then laid her hand on her belly.

"—your baby?" Martha surmised.

Another reluctant nod.

"Oh, Grandma. I'm so sorry. I never knew."

Martha looked at the barren grave, overgrown with weeds. In the church yard, each family was responsible for keeping up the graves of their own departed. Many of the graves had been sadly neglected, and weeds grew up even amid the gravels.

Martha looked again at Mae's sorrowful countenance.

"Well, now." Martha set her mouth in a determined line. "We can do better than this." She painfully knelt down in the gravels at the edge of the tiny grave, and began pulling up the weeds and gathering them to toss over into the peach orchard behind the church. In ten minutes she had the area cleared enough that moss and grass showed through. She looked up at Mae and saw her nod appreciatively.

"We need flowers," Martha declared quietly. She eyed the other vases, as if considering robbing a few here and there. But the flowers were either all plastic and faded into ghastly colors, or else bound in such neat posies she couldn't in good conscience disrupt them. Her eyes glanced over the orchard beyond the church for wild flowers, but found only a few white clovers. Nevertheless, she struck out and picked a cluster of these, along with some peach leaves for greenery, and returned to arrange them as nicely as possible in the little vase.

But observing the results, she frowned. Mae tapped her shoulder and she looked up to see the elderly lady smiling and touching her fingers to her chin in a downward motion that Martha had come to recognize as "thank you."

"Oh, Grandma. You ask so little," Martha whispered to herself, grieved. Then an awareness brightened her face. Something she had overlooked and just now remembered with inspiration.

Martha grasped her Sunday hat and laid it on the ground. Methodically, she ripped the pink silk flowers loose from the band and fitted them into the vase along with the clover. Five silk roses. Perfect! With the white clover and green leaves, it was a beautiful bouquet.

Giving it a final, tender pat, she stood, straightening her skirt and brushing the dirt off of her knees. She heard a little gasp from Mae and looked quickly to see if she was all right. Mae was crying again. But this time with an embarrassed smile behind her hands. She pointed to Martha's ruined hat and shook her head regretfully.

"My pleasure," Martha murmured, giving her a quick hug. "Let's gather the children and go on home."

It was not necessary to enter the church. The brood stood on the church steps, watching in stark astonishment.

"Mama, your hat—" Iris whispered, horrified, as they walked together to the car.

"Shh."

"If I got my church clothes dirty like that—" Nathan speculated.

"Hush up, Nate," his brother said quickly, pushing him towards the car.

The next morning Reuben spent a half hour prying out bent and rusted nails from the old, sagging wood of the back porch steps. He sawed and hammered and sanded. The perspiration dripped from his face and matted his dark bangs.

Reuben, engrossed though he was with his work, became uncomfortably aware of someone studying his every move. Slowly, he looked around behind him.

"Oh—you," he murmured, seeming only slightly relieved. "Where in the world did you come from?" he puzzled. "If you're not the most sneakin' around little kid ever was...."

He struck another blow to the nail balanced between his finger and thumb. "Look, can't you find something better to do," he went on. "I don't cotton much to having folks watch me work. Fact is, I don't cotton much to folks in general. Can't you go play with your little brother or something?"

Her eyes drooped. "I'll be quiet," she whispered.

"It's not that," he said less harshly. "It's just—I'm kind of a loner. I don't like people around while I work. I like to be alone—with just my own thoughts. Focus on getting the job done."

"Loner," Maggie repeated, committing the new word to memory.

"Yeah. I wouldn't be surprised if you're one, too. I've noticed you like to go off by yourself a good bit. So folks'll leave you be."

She made no reply. Her face was expressionless.

"So what you want?" Reuben questioned. "How come you to be out here in the hot sun aggravating me?"

Still she made no comment.

Reuben scratched his hair thoughtfully and wiped the sweat from his face. "Suit yourself," he shrugged. "You're a strange little critter, that's for sure."

He worked awhile in silence. But he was not able to forget that she was there. Irritation built in him. He laid down the hammer and turned full to give her a good stare.

"Say. What's the matter with you, for real, girl? Don't you understand plain English? I don't want you here. Will you please just go away. I have things on my mind. And you're not one of them. And besides, I want to get this here step finished so I can get in out of the hot sun and have me something cool to drink. So just git along somewheres else, will you? Go on, now."

Maggie's face registered only a small degree of hurt. Evidently, Reuben realized, she was accustomed to being spoken to in this way. She only batted her eyes a little and moved her visual focus from her brother to the ground at her feet. Reuben sighed. He felt lousy now. He could see that he had crossed a line, from annoyed to just plain hateful. He hadn't intended that. He jiggled the nails loosely in his left hand, searching for conversation.

"You ever wonder who thought up a thing like nails?" he tossed out, his voice markedly friendlier. No response. "I mean, they're so simple, so almost nothing—and yet they work. You can do amazing things with a hammer and some nails and a few planks of wood." He ventured a look at Maggie. "You know?"

Nothing.

Reuben sighed. He was going to have to either leave this child hurt or take some time to fix the damage he had done. Slowly he thought up some words. "People used to build whole houses with not much more than what I'm holding right here, that's a fact. Well, it took a lot more wood than this, of course." He waited. The silence was beginning to unnerve him. He picked out a good straight nail and hammered it in place, securing the board. All that remained now was to fasten several more nails in a straight line, to solidly secure it in a 90-degree angle to the board below. There would be no more tripping or stumbling for his family coming up and down these stairs.

"When I was—well—the place where I worked before this," the boy caught himself, "they told me I had a natural knack for wood-working. I got to study about it in shop. Made a lamp that looked just like a little wooden pump. And it worked. When you raised up the lever, like you would to pump water, a real light bulb came on." He smiled a fraction at the memory. "Wonder what ever become of that lamp?"

Again he looked at Maggie, sure that this story would have caught her interest. She was looking at his face, but her own face revealed nothing.

"Maybe I can remember—I'm not promising anything, now—but I *might* can remember how, and make another one with the scraps left over after I finish this job. And then I could give it to you. To keep. Would you like that?"

171

He barely heard her whisper: "Yes."

Reuben swallowed hard. Whatever was wrong with his little sister, he was not making it better. Her extreme shyness pierced his heart. He resolved to be more patient with her. Try to bring her out a little.

"I think I'm gonna call you Magpie," the young man said, managing, with effort, a small crooked grin. "On account of you talk so much."

Maggie looked at him, seriously puzzled.

He sighed. His smile drooped.

"You know, like that bird, the magpie? Squawks and jabbers all the time? Well, it's a joke, see. 'Cause fact is, you don't hardly never talk at all. It's supposed to be ironic—" he shook his head, knowing that word would be meaningless to her. "It's supposed to be funny. Kinda." Well, that was a bust, he berated himself.

Reuben laid down his hammer on the step and studied his newly acquainted little sister, while jiggling nails in his left hand.

"What's the matter with you, anyhow, Maggie?" he asked bluntly, though not unkindly. "How come you're so—" he hesitated, careful of his wording. "Nobody else in this family is slow or nothing. It ain't about that, though, is it." It was an observation, not a question. "You can talk. You just don't want to talk." He threw the theory out there, to see how she would respond. Only she didn't respond at all. She reached into the bucket and pulled out a handful of nails.

"No, now—quit that." Reuben took her by the wrist and shook the nails loose. "Nails ain't no kinda plaything for a little girl. You'll poke a hole in your hand, if you're not careful. Don't you have a dolly or something to mess with?"

This time Maggie nodded somberly.

"Well. Go get that, how about? You can hold your dolly and watch me work if you want. Just stay on the porch, out of my way."

The child stood and obediently wandered inside the house.

Reuben bit the inside of his cheek. Now look, you done hurt the kid's feelings again. But she was safer away from his labor. You never knew when something like a nail might skew off and hit somebody. He measured and hammered another nail into the blonde wood. Then he sat back on his heels and studied the contrast between the warped grey middle step and this crisp new plank of lumber. Daddy had not allowed him to buy all fresh lumber. Only the two pieces to fix the stair that was completely broken in two, and the badly warped one. It was going to be ugly as the dickens, he judged, shaking his head. Well, it wasn't his house and never would be. He wasn't the same as real family anymore—not to his father, anyhow. The house would go to Sonny someday. And that suited him fine. He didn't much like this old house. There were more hurtful memories here than happy ones. He thought of Bo's plan to leave the state, drive up through North Carolina and into Virginia. Bo said Virginia was pretty land, and the Appalachian Mountains made for lots of safe places to hide out awhile. He blinked into the sun, lost in sobering thoughts.

The screen door creaked and softly closed. He twisted his body to look behind him, and a small trace of a sad smile passed over his mouth.

Maggie stepped toward him, carefully holding a large glass of water literally crowded with ice cubes. She extended this offering to Reuben with both hands, without a word.

He received it, hesitating, feeling strangely unworthy. "Thank you."

She turned away without comment and went back up on the porch. She had brought her ragged doll Nellie downstairs. Making not a sound, she sat in the shadows of the porch, far out of Reuben's way. Holding the doll sitting straight up in her lap, she sat primly atop the cast off mattress. She sat with legs stretched out, her feet together, watching him work. They might have been two dolls, set one on top of the other, she kept so still.

Reuben drank the water greedily, without pause, then belched. He set the glass of ice on the grass and half-heartedly sanded the board a little more, struck another nail in and then seemed to wait for something. His head was bent forward, as if the boy were weary to his soul. Then he straightened up and looked back at his sister.

"Hey, Maggie. You want I should teach you a little bit about wood-working?"

She gazed at him blankly.

He tried again. "Do you want to try hammering in one of these nails, like you seen me do?"

In her subdued way, she was instantly alert. She nodded quickly.

"C'mere, then."

She laid Nellie carefully down on the mattress and almost simultaneously was at his side.

"Okay, now, you can't throw a fit if you mash your finger, understand? That's gonna happen now and again. But hold the nail like this, and there's less chance of it. Take the hammer in your other hand and strike that nail head a lick. You don't have to hit it hard, just straight."

Maggie gave the wide nail head a delicate tap. It didn't go in, but it didn't go crooked, either.

Reuben grinned. "There you go. That's the way. Try again, a little bit harder."

She obeyed and the nail sank into the wood a fraction of an inch.

Reuben tousled her hair. "Well, look at you! I swear if you ain't a natural-born carpenter."

Maggie smiled shyly, and Reuben thought his heart had stopped beating. So she *could* smile.

"Go again," he nodded toward the nail. His voice came out in a husky whisper and he cleared his throat self-consciously. He watched in silence as Maggie gently hammered the nail again and again, until it was flush with the wood—his moist eyes fixed not on her hands but on her focused face.

Part Four

Monday night Lester came home late from work. He was too tired even to eat supper, he told Martha. The children had eaten earlier and were already in bed.

"Just fix me a cup of coffee," he said with a soul-deep sigh.

She brought him the coffee and stood behind his chair, rubbing his sore shoulders with a sweet slow touch.

"Woman...that feels like heaven," Lester murmured, leaning his head back into her hands. She massaged his damp temples with practiced fingertips.

"What happened today, Les?" she asked.

He shook his head. "Peaches just filled right out after that rain the other day. It's like they all ripened at once, round and firm and juicy. Not enough pickers.

Mr. Johnson even had some of the ladies from the shed out in the fields picking and loading like migrants, for a little while. They weren't none too happy about it, either. But you know how it is, workin' in peaches. Everybody has got to do whatever is needed, whenever it's needed. Mr. Johnson don't put up with no foolishness. Anyhow, it wasn't long until they were needed worse in the shed and he moved 'em back."

Lester opened his blue eyes wide and looked up into his wife's face. "He did give a bonus to some of us. Like me—for working seventeen hours straight. He's fair, I'll give him that. He appreciates a loyal employee. I told him I'd bring the boys in with me tomorrow, to help out. You think Jackson's grown enough to put in a whole day? I'm not talking about overtime. Not at thirteen."

"You can ask him, honey."

"They're all asleep I reckon."

Lester sipped at his steaming coffee. "Mm. I got so hungry out there, Martha, I ate peaches 'til I swear I hope I never have to taste another peach as long as I live! Besides which I ate 'em, hungry or not, just to keep my strength up."

Martha laughed mildly. "Do I need to pack two lunches for you? I do believe."

"No way of knowing, when I go in, how many hours I'll be gone. Like last week when I got a half-day off, with pay. I'll get by on my sandwiches and those blasted culls."

"Thought you were never gonna eat another peach as long as—"

"Well, that might be a long ol' time. I might have to eat some words along in there, too." He smiled and she gave him a grateful hug. She knew the smile didn't come easy, with his muscles so sore and his soul tired to the bone.

"I got some biscuits left over from supper, Les, would that be good with your coffee?"

His eyebrows lifted. "That sounds real fine, now you mention it. Easy on my stomach, too."

He laid his head on the table for the brief moments it took her to warm the biscuits over. She wrapped each one in a damp paper towel to keep them moist and tender. Then she quickly buttered four and set them, along with a jar of jelly, on a plate by his coffee mug. In those few minutes he had fallen lightly asleep. The quiet tap of the plate and jar being set down on the table top was sufficient to rouse him.

"Huh? I was already in the middle of a crazy dream," he remarked with sleepy surprise, sitting up. "I hate to come in so late I miss seeing my children morning *and* night," Lester fretted. "They'll likely grow up rememberin' me as the fella that was away at work all the time and only came home to holler at 'em."

Martha only smiled. She sat beside him at the table.

He groaned a little, pleasurably, tasting the warm bread.

"Have you talked to Maggie about you maybe home-schoolin' her come fall?" Les inquired thickly through a full mouth.

"Not yet. I wanted to be completely sure it was all right by you before I got Maggie's hopes up."

He nodded, chewing.

"I'm anxious to tell her, though," Martha mused with a tender smile. "She'll be so happy, Les. And don't think I'm being sassy, but I honestly believe I can teach her better here at home. She needs little rests and breaks during the day; and she'll be able to pay attention better without noise from the other kids, whispering and giggling and such. And I understand her, leastwise as much as anybody can. I know when to push for a little more, and when she's got no more to give. I believe I can get her up to grade, Les.

I really want to try. I don't want to send her back there to have Mrs. Sanders another year."

"You got your hands awful full without teaching, Martha," her husband reminded her.

"But a lot of my work is tiresome, Les, like yours can be. Thinking about teaching Maggie makes me feel happy. I get ideas for projects we can do, and books we can read together—and I—I actually feel young again. I think I'll have more energy."

"Well, I say we give it a try. And as long as it pleases you, we'll keep on. If you get tired or find it's wearing you down, then we can see about putting her back in school."

Martha laid her hand over his. "Thank you, Les."

He nodded. "Well, you can go ahead and tell her. I won't change my mind. I think it'll be for the best; and I think you'll be the prettiest little school marm ever was."

Impulsively she hugged him. " I'll do a good job, you'll see."

Lester smiled. "I know you will. I'm not worried about that.'Preciate you staying up for me, by the way," he added, starting on the third biscuit. I know you're awful tired, too."

"I'm all right. Les, do you want me to come help out with the peaches tomorrow, too? I haven't forgotten how. Bring in some extra money?"

He shook his head. "Naw. I considered it, but if you go Jackson would have to stay to watch over the little ones. Let's give Jackson a crack at earning his own money. I believe he'll cotton to it."

Steps on the stairs, sock-feet, caught their attention.

"Well, somebody's up," Martha acknowledged. "And here it is going on one o'clock in the morning."

"Oh, don't tell me that, baby, I got to get up at five," Lester groaned.

Out of the dimness of the stairway, Reuben appeared, disheveled and barely awake. He scratched at the night stubble on his chin and jaws, which irritated him between shaves. "Everybody up?" he questioned with an inadvertent frown against the bright light of the kitchen. "Is it mornin' already?"

"Just us, dear," his mother replied. "I fixed your daddy a late-night snack; would you like some coffee and biscuits?"

"No'm. Thanks. I just need a glass of water—I'll get it myself," he added quickly as his mother started to rise.

Lester spoke. "Son, we're low on workers and off-the-charts on work at the orchard. I'm asking Sonny and Jackson to come out to the fields with me tomorrow to work. I need you to come, too. Mr. Johnson told me to bring anybody I knew of that would like to earn a few dollars spending-money. I reckon that would suit all you boys pretty fine?"

Reuben rinsed a glass at the sink and filled it with water. He drank it at the sink, peering out the window at the flowing black outline of the trees against the charcoal sky. There was a moon tonight, intermittently hidden by clouds that passed overhead in swift procession, portending rain. The wind was up a little. It rustled the leaves on the maple trees, creating a rushing sound, full of whispers.

Carefully, without turning, he framed his response. "Daddy, I kind of had in mind to start painting the house tomorrow. I'm real anxious to make it look good again. Sonny picked up the paint in town: pure white, semi-gloss. It's gonna be real pretty."

"Well, good. That sounds mighty fine. That can wait, though, and the peaches can't. I need you and your brothers in the fields tomorrow. Sonny can drive a refrigerated truck and a Hyster like nobody's business. We'll probably put Jackson to pickin'."

Reuben hesitated. His heart was pounding. He poured more water into his glass and drank it slowly.

"Looks like might be some rain tomorrow," he casually mentioned.

"Callin' for it in the late afternoon. That's another reason Mr.Johnson wants to get an early start with all the workers we can round up. Any money you earn will be yours to keep or spend. Can I count on you, son?"

Reuben swallowed all the water in the glass before making an answer.

"I'll be up and dressed," he said quietly. "I'll be ready. What time you leaving out?"

"No later than five-thirty."

Reuben smiled slightly. "You think Jackson can be up by then?"

"I'll wake him up. He'll be glad for the money. Plus, it'll be good experience for him. A couple more years and he'll be hired on at the peach shed, summers."

Reuben nodded, half-listening. "Mama, would you come wake me up early?"

"Sure."

"Guess I'd better get back to bed then, while I can," he nodded. With shy eyes, he cast a glance over the faces of both his parents. " Daddy. Mama. I've not had a chance to tell you, what with the kids around all the time. But I appreciate everything. All your kindness to me. More than I got words to say. I just want you to know that."

Lester nodded approvingly, and Martha crossed over to give her son a warm hug. "We love you, Reuben," she murmured.

"I know. And I don't deserve—"

"Shh," she interrupted him gently. "Sleep well, now, you hear? Nothing but sweet dreams."

"Yes'm," he answered with a nostalgic smile. The tender, familiar words seemed to him like something remembered from another lifetime.

Reuben set down his glass in the sink and turned back toward the stairs.

Early in the morning, in the pre-dawn darkness, Martha knocked on the door to Reuben's room. The door wasn't latched and swung easily open under the light weight of her hand.

"Reuben?" she questioned, straining to see in the darkness.

Her vision cleared, only to make her heart sink.

The bed was made. The backpack with its contents, Reuben's pitiful store of belongings, was gone. The bedroom was unbearably empty, sickening in the grey of morning light.

Martha sat down on the neatly spread cot. "Oh, Reuben, Reuben," she whispered, her throat constricting with aching tears. This was Lester's fault, she thought bitterly, for trying to put Reuben to work with a bunch of other folks. He wasn't ready. She would have known better. But there wasn't time for any emotion this morning, Martha told herself sternly. She roused from her thoughts to go downstairs and wake her other sons.

It was then, as she stood, that she saw the note. Hastily grabbing it up, she turned on the bedside lamp. She scanned the words with blurred eyes.

"Mama, I'm sorry. I have to meet that fellow today. You remember? Tell Daddy I'm sorry, and also I'm sorry I wasn't man enough to tell him to his face. I'll be back someday, Mama, if I can. I promise. Love, Reuben."

Martha held the note so hard against her chest that she crumpled it. She had no prayer for this. She merely sobbed, in aching silent spasms. Later she would find words for all that was in her heart. Later she would let herself cry aloud.

For now, she must dry her face and steady herself, to go and wake up Jackson. She must pack lunches for a boy and two men. She must send them off with a smile and, most likely, a comfortable lie for the time being.

Two days passed. Questions about Reuben were again forbidden. Lester insisted it be that way. The children were simply told he had to be somewhere and hoped to return soon. The younger ones had many questions, but

Martha instructed them not to ask, and they obeyed. There was a strained curiosity in the house for several days, and then all settled, more or less, back to normal.

In private, Lester berated his second born son to Martha, who listened patiently. She simply listened quietly, understanding that Lester was, in his own way, as hurt as she was herself. As disappointed at losing Reuben again.

Her mind wandered, as her husband grumbled. She was picturing her men-folk playing checkers on the front porch, recent evenings. They'd had play-offs sometimes. Sonny against Lester. Lester against Reuben. And there had been laughter between them lately—not much, but some.

Lester concluded his tirade and then he was calmer. After a pause he said, "I'm sorry for your sake, Martha."

She nodded her appreciation, not trusting her voice.

"Nothing will ever be the same," Lester mused. "There won't be another second chance for Reuben. It's over."

"Maybe—"

"It's over, Martha."

After a few seconds she cleared her throat. "I'd better check on the washing," she murmured, leaving the room.

If Martha expected Maggie to be ecstatic over the news of home-schooling, she was unhappily mistaken. The little girl took in the words with a blank, expressionless face. She asked a few questions, as if negotiating.

"Can I have Percy with me?" she wanted to know.

"We'll see. Maybe we can have Percy join us in school when you do extra good," Mama compromised.

"Will Nathan be in regular school?"

"Yes, he's five now. He'll be in school a half day. That's when we'll get most of our school work done."

"You'll be my teacher?"

Mama smiled. "Yes! Me. Won't that be fun?"

For the first time Maggie smiled a little, shyly.

"You want to stay home with Mama for school?" Martha pressed.

A pause. An almost indifferent, "Yes."

Her mother sighed. This was all the enthusiasm she was going to get. She scolded herself for wanting and needing more. Well, she would have to provide it herself, she decided.

"It's going to be the best school in the whole wide world!" she assured Maggie.

"It is?" The little girl's eyes opened wide.

"For us, it is. I can teach you things you'll love to learn, in ways you'll enjoy learning....arithmetic, reading, spelling...." she paused, knowing she had lost Maggie's attention already. "With God's help," she sighed, her hopes drooping just a little. "It'll be fine, Maggie-Muffin."

Now the child grinned, "I'm not a muffin," she protested playfully. "Iris calls me that all the time. But I'm not."

"It's a nickname—a play-name," Mama explained to this most literal child.

"Nobody else has a play- name."

"Sure they do. Sonny's real name is Lester Joseph Burnett, Junior."

Now the blue eyes opened wide. "It is?"

"It is. See, I just taught you something already, and school hasn't even started yet!" On this encouraged note Martha returned to the kitchen with happy plans for future lessons.

One Friday evening in early July, Maggie finished helping wash the dishes and disappeared. Nine o'clock came, darkness was falling, and the child was still unaccounted for. Jackson had been dispatched to search outside the house for her, with no luck.

Martha began to be frantic—until she looked in the doorway of the front bedroom and found Grandma rocking and tunelessly humming in the chair by her bed, with Maggie very nearly asleep in her lap.

The worry in Martha's eyes softened. For a moment she just stood outside the door and watched, arms folded, letting her heart settle. Letting anger drain.

Then she tiptoed quietly into the room. "Isn't she too heavy for you, Grandma?"

Mae shook her head firmly.

"Maggie," Mama said, leaning over her. "It's time for bed, now."

Mae looked at Martha wistfully. It was a mother's look, a grandmother's look, that of a woman who has not held a child in a very long time.

Maggie raised sleepy eyes to her mother's face, waiting.

"All right," Mama said slowly. "But just for a little. Grandma, you mustn't let my children wear you out, now, you hear? They'll do it if you let them."

Much later that night, Maggie woke in her own bed, thirsty.

She walked sleepily to the stairs and started down.

But at the landing her footsteps slowed.

There was a light in the living room. It was not the lamp. This light was a circle, almost like a firefly, but brighter— moving restlessly over the cabinet in the corner.

She was too sleepy to be frightened, but the quivering round light, changing constantly in size and location roused her curiosity. She eased herself down the last six steps and stood watching from the dark.

Whispers came to her ears. Quick, frustrated words that she couldn't make out. But she recognized one of the voices.

"Reuben?" she said softly.

The light instantly swung to her face, stinging her eyes like a slap. She raised one hand quickly, to shade them from the brightness.

"—Maggie?" Reuben said in a guarded voice. "What you doin' up, girl?"

"I need a drink of water."

"Well, get it," the voice said in a guarded whisper. "And hurry up on back to bed."

But Maggie didn't go to the kitchen. Instead, she took a step closer to the source of the light. Toward her brother, she thought.

A sudden, dirty hand snatched out from behind the flashlight and grabbed her face, covering her mouth.

The girl tried to cry out for her mother, but could only gasp, "Unh—!"

The crushing hand, damp and smelling of sweat and metal, clamped her mouth still tighter.

She felt something strike hard against the arm that held her. "Let go of her! That's my sister—!" It was Reuben's voice.

"Shut up, you—" returned the stranger.

The space around Maggie became filled with furiously whispered threats and curses. "Let go, I told you—!"

"Back off, Burnett!"

"If anything—!"

"Back off, I said!"

"Not until you—"

"Wait!—just wait—just —*wait.*"

Sudden quiet fell. The flashlight was softly snapped off. The darkness that replaced it was strangely comforting. Pale moonlight from the bare window coaxed the constricted pupils of Maggie's eyes to enlarge. Gradually the forms of two men became dimly visible. Their whisperings were too low, now, for her to comprehend. The stranger still had a tight hold on her.

Then Reuben bent down on one knee in front of her. He spoke calmly, now, altogether differently. "Maggie, this here is Bo. He's a friend of mine, okay? He's gonna turn you loose now. But you got to promise you won't holler, y' understand?"

With the iron grip of Bo's hand still across her mouth, Maggie tried to nod.

"You promise, then?" Reuben persisted. "Cross your heart?"

She nodded again.

Bo released her, begrudgingly, with a muttered curse. She drew a deep breath of clean air, and rubbed her mouth with the back of her hand, trying to wipe off the filthy smudge of his hardened fingers.

"Maggie-girl," Reuben said in a low voice. "You got to help us out, now. We got to borrow some cash. Where's Mama keep the grocery money? She used to keep it here in the cabinet. But it ain't here no more."

The girl looked from her brother's face to the dark, scowling face of his accomplice. "You can't take—"

"Shh! Keep your voice down!" the man called Bo scolded in a fierce whisper.

Reuben thought fast. "All's we need is about three dollars. For gas. For the car. And we'll pay it back, okay? It's real important, Magsie."

Maggie hesitated. In the darkness Bo cursed her again. Reuben touched her arm. "Come on, now. Nobody's gonna hurt you, but you got to tell, you understand?"

Maggie murmured, "It's in the kitchen. In the blue coffee can."

Reuben disappeared with the flashlight.

In the living room, Bo's hand closed smoothly around Maggie's thin neck. "Don't you make a sound, you hear?" he growled. "If you even sneeze, I'll—"

Reuben was back in an instant, the flashlight propped between his elbow and ribs while he hastily counted the bills.

"I make it out to be around forty-seven dollars," he muttered to Bo.

"You're lying. That isn't worth the walk over here. There's got to be more somewhere."

"My folks are poor," Reuben reminded him. "I told you that. This is actually better'n I figured on."

"Well, the car's the main thing we need, anyhow."

Maggie spoke. "You said—"

Bo clamped his hand hard around her throat. She could feel his fingertips bruising the delicate, tender places in her neck beneath the skin. "Don't—" she gasped. Her tiny fingers helplessly tugged, trying to pull his crushing hand away.

"You ain't nothin' to me girl, I'd as soon kill you as look at you," he hissed.

"Stop scaring her!" Reuben demanded. "There's no need for that." To Maggie he said gently, "You did real good. I'm proud of you. Do you need me to walk with you back up to bed?"

"You can't do that," Bo snarled. "Somebody'll hear you. What're you thinking? Come on, we gotta get out of here, man! We gotta figure what to do with the kid."

"Let her go, I told you."

Bo shook his head menacingly. "She'll wake up the whole house, the minute we're out the door. If you got rope and duct tape, we can tie her up and gag her—or we can take her along as a hostage."

Reuben swore. "Shut up that kind of talk," he whispered furiously, "I told you, don't be scaring her!"

Bo's lowered voice came out soft, measured, cold. "I'm not saying it to scare her. I'm saying it because we got to do something fast." He hesitated, letting Reuben try to think. Then he added, "the smart thing would be for me to just snap her neck like a twig. She'd never make a sound."

Reuben stared at him in unmitigated shock. "I can't—I can't believe—that you —would even—" he managed to stammer. The words shook out of his mouth raggedly like broken black scraps from a pepper mill.

For the first time, Bo showed the handgun which he had kept hidden inside his jacket. He brought it out smoothly, like a prize. The white moonlight glinted off the polished metal, bright as the sun. "I don't want to use this at the moment, because of the noise it would make." Bo twirled the gun with a low chuckle, then tucked it away, out of sight. "But you need to know that I got it."

"Fine. Just leave, man," Reuben said in defeat. "Take the car, take the money. Just leave us be."

Bo sighed. "Sorry. No can do. You better go on out to the car, Rube. I don't need no help with this."

He tightened his grip on the child's neck, and she made a desperate, nearly inaudible cry.

With a curse, Reuben punched Bo across the jaw, and as he did the heavy flashlight fell and struck the bare wood floor with a resounding thud.

Both men froze.

"Get outta here!" Bo commanded Reuben in a husky whisper. "*Now*!"

Bo picked up Maggie with one arm and shoved both of them ahead of him, out into the dark night.

In the front bedroom, Mae Burnett's eyes flew open. She had wakened suddenly, frightened, her heart pounding. She listened hard to the night.

There was not a sound anywhere, except the faint, peaceful stirrings of frogs and crickets. But she had heard something.

It might have been a dream, she reasoned. She closed her eyes and tried to calm herself.

Then another sound came. This one subdued and stealthy. A crunching of tires over gravel—like a moving car—but without any noise from a motor.

Mae sat up in bed and pulled aside her window curtain. A bulky, dark shape was moving through the deeper darkness outside. It was a car. Both front doors were wide open, and two men were pushing the car out of the driveway in almost perfect silence.

Mae struggled to get out of bed. Her body felt heavy to her, and difficult to manage, and the bedclothes seemed to wrap and knot themselves around her like the stubborn tendrils of clinging vines.

"Help"—she tested the word in her mind, and then tried to call out, but her voice emitted a sound no louder than the squeal of a mouse, tiny and frail.

She managed at last to get to her feet, and located her cane propped against the night stand. With it she steadied herself, and made her way to the bedroom door.

She came out into the moonlit hall and stood at the foot of the stairs, her face turned upward in desperation.

Again she called out with all the strength she could muster. Still she couldn't make herself heard.

She looked woefully at the steeply rising stairs, knowing she could not possibly climb them alone. Tears came into her eyes.

Nevertheless, bravely, she raised one foot, and placed it on the first step. Then she pushed herself up, clinging to the rail and leaning on her cane. Another step. Her whole body trembled. It was no use. She stumbled back down to the level floor, grabbing at the stair rail to keep from falling altogether.

Albert and Iris, coming in long overdue from their date, met a car going much too fast for the bumpy condition of the dirt back road. The young couple squinted their eyes at the glaring headlights defiantly set on bright.

"We're not the only ones high-tailing it home," Albert remarked with a glance in his girlfriend's direction.

Iris had twisted around in her seat, trying to see the car before it disappeared in the night. "That looked—kinda looked—like my Daddy's car," she told Albert, alarmed. "You don't think—surely he wouldn't have gone out huntin' us because—what time is it, anyhow?"

Albert shrugged. "You don't want to know, Baby. It's late."

"Oh no! I am gonna get killed! I mean, *killed*! Killed dead," Iris gasped.

"Naw, you're just imagining things 'cause you know we're late. Your folks are sound asleep at home, I guarantee."

"You just better *hope* my Mama and Daddy are asleep," Iris told him fervently.

Albert eased the car into the front yard and leaned to kiss Iris goodnight, but she was staring into the empty yard in consternation.

"Daddy's car is gone," she managed to say, already starting to cry. She unlatched the door on her side and leapt out, trembling. She ran toward the porch steps without a backward glance. Albert followed. Catching up with her, he grabbed her elbow before she could open the front door.

"You're not gonna face this alone. I do care about you, Iris, you don't believe me sometimes, but I do. I'm gonna stay right here until we find out what's the deal."

Iris's face softened. Her lips brushed his face. She pointed to one of the porch rocking chairs. "Just sit there. I'll come back and tell you whatever I find out." She hesitated. "If Daddy has gone lookin' for me, I might get you to take me to Suzy's house for the night. Give him time to cool down."

The boy nodded agreement.

"But you need to be gone before he gets back," she added emphatically. Once inside the house, Iris slipped off her high heels and walked quickly, silently toward the stairs. She stepped over the flashlight in the living room floor, without taking note of it.

In her hurry, she nearly ran headlong into Mae. The sight of her great-grandmother standing ghost-like in the moonlit hallway gave Iris a shock.

"Grandma!" she exclaimed, laying a hand over her racing heart. "What in the world are you—what's going on, Grandma—did Daddy go out huntin' me?—oh, Grandma—I'm so late gettin' home, he's totally gonna kill me! What am I gonna do—?"

Mae shook her head firmly. She pressed both hands against her right cheek, conveying sleep.

"They're asleep?" Iris repeated, hardly daring to believe it. "But—but—the car—?"

Iris had no chance to say anything more. The older lady grasped her arm frantically, pouring out a breathless torrent of whispered broken syllables as she pointed up the stairs.

"I don't understand, Grandma, you want me to wake them up? Grandma, I can't, they'll—"

Mae made an effort to slow her broken communication. She pointed toward the front yard, whispering, "Car."

"I know. The car's gone. That's why I thought—" Iris suddenly comprehended what her grandmother had said. The impact hit her full force. "Somebody stole my Daddy's car?"

Mae nodded her head, desperately. She tried to explain further. Her own words infuriated her, coming as they did in senseless, breathy bits and pieces.

Grandma! Are you all right? Nobody hurt you did they?"

Mae dismissed that notion with a little wave of her hand.

Iris breathed the sigh of relief.

Again Mae pointed upstairs.

"Yes, I'll wake them up, just—give me a minute."

She led Mae back to her bed. "You lie down, now, and don't worry. It'll be okay. Don't get yourself all worked up, Grandma, you might make yourself sick. Okay?"

Mae nodded, calmer now that Iris was here to help.

Satisfied, Iris came back out of Mae's room and looked up the stairs anxiously. Everything was quiet. Everyone was asleep.

In nearly perfect silence, the girl ran up the stairs to her room, her high-heeled shoes in her hand. She pushed her shoes under her bed, hidden. With trembling, hurried fingers she peeled off her daytime clothes, shoved them into the closet, jerked her hand-me-down bathrobe off the hanger and wrapped it around her, tying it in a knot.

The room was dimly bright from the full moon shining through the open window.

Iris faced the mirror over her dresser and mussed her hair, then wiped her face clean of make-up with a soiled blouse that was lying on top of the dresser. Only then, as she turned to leave, ready to go wake her parents, did she see that the bed across the room was empty, the covers tossed back.

"No!" she cried, "Not Maggie—!"

Part Five

The Buick careened along the back roads at breakneck speed. Reuben, against his will, was at the wheel. The muscles in his arms and jaws were taut and hard as rocks. Bo lounged against the passenger-side window, as if he had been born and raised in a get-away car.

In the back seat, Maggie clung to the arm-rest of her door with one hand and the edge of the seat with the other.

The car bounded over a red mud gully and landed at the edge of a paved road.

"Well, finally," Reuben breathed out his relief.

A mile or so further and they were on the Asheville Highway, headed toward downtown Spartanburg. As they entered the city, rows of street lamps on each side of the road poured round puddles of watery white light onto the asphalt.

Maggie sat up straighter and peered out her window. There was not another moving car anywhere in sight.

It seemed eerie to Maggie, how all that light was pouring down only for them—and after they drove by, it kept pouring down, just in case someone else might come along before morning. She turned herself sideways and watched out the back window, to see if any other cars would come, or a policeman, or even a stray dog or cat—but no one came. No one at all. There were just those rows of street lamps, pouring out their hopeful brightness, free and ready, in case anyone was in need of light. It made Maggie feel strange and lonely and deeply sad.

Darkness, she thought, would have been better. Plain dark. She felt sorry for the light, so giving and so all alone.

"What time is it?" she asked.

Bo turned and looked at her. "You don't need to know that."

Reuben said, "Around three, three-thirty."

Maggie settled back against the seat. " I've never been up this late," she mused aloud.

Bo grunted disparagingly.

"That so," Reuben mumbled. This revelation held scarcely more fascination for her brother, evidently, than it did for his comrade.

Maggie's meager moment of self-importance waned. She leaned her head back against the seat, watching the ghostly buildings, billboards and trees that streaked by her window. She found herself growing tired and wanting her mother. But it would be useless to mention it, she knew without needing to be told. She lay down on the seat and tried to sleep, but the car was chilly in the night air, and she was still in her cotton nightgown.

She sat up. "I'm cold," she announced cautiously.

Reuben looked at Bo. "I told you you'd be sorry," he muttered.

"Ain't this car got a heater?" Bo demanded with a grimace.

"Yeah."

"Well, shut up and turn the thing on, then. And you—" he said, craning his neck to look at Maggie in the back seat. "You shut up, too. You-all are treadin' on my nerves bad, the both of you."

Maggie lay back down, tucking her nightgown around her as snugly as she could.

In a few minutes the car began to be warm. The rocking motion lulled her into a half-sleep, so that the voices from the front seat seemed to be weaving in and out of some strange dream.

"Where we meeting the others?" Reuben's voice sounded vague and far away.

Bo answered with an exaggerated southern accent. "The Stardust Mo-tell, my man. Kobra's done got a room and waitin' on us."

"What we need a room for? If you ask me, we need to put some serious miles between us and this neck of the woods, fast."

"Well nobody asked you, did they?" Bo said smoothly. He laid his head back against the head-rest with a sardonic trace of a smile and watched the dark landscape through tired and narrowed eyes.

Lester fought to wake himself, alarmed by Iris's presence and her shrill, agitated words.

When he got the gist of the hysteria he sent her downstairs and pulled on his daytime khaki's and T-shirt. He flung his shoes on without tying them.

"Les, wait for me," Martha pleaded, pulling on her slippers. "I want to go too."

But Les was already halfway downstairs. He pointed a stern finger at Iris. "I'll talk to you later." Then with narrowed eyes, he thrust his open palm out to Albert. "You—! Boy—! Gimme your keys!" Albert didn't argue. He handed over the key to his Chevy as if it were hot and he was glad to be rid of it.

Lester said nothing else to anyone. He ran to Albert's car, jerked the door open and cranked the engine. The car roared out of the driveway and onto the road.

Martha stood in her bathrobe with one slipper on and one in her hand. "Oh, Lord, God," she prayed.

Out on the road Lester drove the speed limit until he woke up enough to think what he was doing. He cursed himself for a fool. He needed a cop to stop him, and to help him. He revved the car up to ninety, as fast as it would go.

It wasn't long until he heard a siren. Thankfully he pulled over and started to get out of the car. But the policeman who had stopped behind him dropped to one knee with his gun aimed straight at Lester. "Don't get out of your car!" he yelled.

"My little girl has been kidnapped and my car was stolen," Les said in a blur of words.

"Get back in your car! Now!"

Nothing was going to happen until he obeyed. He sat in the driver's seat, fuming.

At a snail's pace the cop crept toward him, still with his gun aimed.

"Officer, my little daughter has been kidnapped and my car was stolen. Please help me."

"Put your hands together behind your head and step slowly out."

Lester did as he was told.

"Now put your hands on the car and spread your legs."

The officer frisked him, then asked for his driver's license.

"We're losing valuable time, officer," Les pointed out. His nostrils flared.

The other man finished looking over the license and handed it back to Les. The cop went to his car and spoke with headquarters on the two-way radio. It seemed to Lester that they talked for ten minutes or more. He thought he would lose his mind, waiting.

Then the cop signaled for him to come get in the patrol car.

"HQ had already put out a BOLO. There's been a sighting on a car that fits your description," he said calmly, starting the motor. "Speeding. But the policeman was off duty and didn't go after him. Just reported it. We'll go in that direction."

Lester bowed his head in his hands

The cop gave him a slight nod. "We'll get your car *and* your young'un back."

"Thank you," Les mumbled.

As they neared downtown Spartanburg, another police car crossed their path.

The cop made a quick turn and followed the other car, simultaneously talking into the radio to headquarters.

"They sighted your car, too." the cop explained, accelerating. "Hold on. We're going to speed it up a bit. This time of night there aren't many cars on the road. They won't get away."

Reuben, Maggie and Bo were well into the city, now, keeping a good speed along the empty streets.

The trees turned a preternatural green in the glare of the Buick's headlights, and then drained black again as the car swept by.

Maggie, awake now and sitting up, got that same sickened feeling she'd had before. As if they had gotten the trees' hopes up for nothing, and disappointed them, just like the street lamps. She tried to reason with herself that trees and lanterns don't have feelings. But she wasn't convinced of that. And the scary sadness wouldn't go away.

Maggie began to cry softly.

Bo rolled down his window to toss out a cigarette. The tiny stub ripped through the cold air, trailing red-orange sparks of fire, brilliant against the black of the night. The cold air made a sudden rush in and whipped Maggie's pale, loose hair around her face like a flag in high winds.

"And— here we are!" Bo announced suddenly. "Turn in up ahead there, Rube. Yep. Right there."

Maggie pushed the hair out of her eyes and looked.

There was a muddle of lights ahead of them on the right. As they drew closer, the lights separated into a gas station that appeared to be open, but wasn't, a diner that may or may not have been closed—and a slightly run-down motel with a neon sign flashing the word "Stardust." Below that sign, a red neon light spelled out "Vacancies—Yes." Above it, tiny neon stars spewed out in all directions, perched atop visible wires.

"Classy," Reuben noted darkly. Bo laughed out loud.

Reuben pulled in, glancing nervously at the few cars in the parking lot. "Which room?" he muttered.

"Over there," his friend said, pointing. "That's Kobra's truck, the red and white one. That'll be his room, there—the one with the light on."

Maggie sat up straight, straining to see. Yes, one room was still lighted at this hour. Two heavy curtains covered the entire window, but from the narrow crevice where the curtains joined, a thread of yellow light pierced the darkness like a hot, buttered knife.

Reuben parked beside the red and white truck. He exhaled a weary sigh.

"What'sa matter with you?" Bo demanded.

Reuben didn't answer him.

Bo turned half around in the seat. "Get out," he instructed Maggie.

She was suddenly afraid. She looked at her brother and realized that she barely knew him well enough to call him by name. Reuben was staring straight ahead, lost in his own thoughts.

Bo scowled at her with an angry curse, twisted fully around and jerked her door handle open from the inside. "Get out, I told you!"

Maggie all but fell out of the car. The door, as if of its own accord, shut behind her.

She stood motionless on the black pavement, shivering, waiting. The two men inside the car talked in low, argumentative voices. She could not clearly hear what they were saying. Fast syllables. Agitation. Maggie hung her head, wishing for her doll Nellie to hold. She dared not wish for Mama. That would make her cry.

The night air was unseasonably chilled. The cold, together with fear, made her tremble, and long for her sweater. She rubbed her hands up and down along her arms, glancing uneasily from the car window to the single one-note shriek of light from the rented motel room, and out again to the highway, where the occasional streaking headlights of an unseen car flew by in the dark.

After a minute, Reuben and Bo both got out of the car. They stared at the door of the motel room where the man named Kobra was holed up, and looked with apprehension at one another. There was a feeling in the air of something not right.

"Knock," Bo directed, nodding his head toward the door.

"You knock," Reuben said sullenly, his dark face half-hidden under the bank of brown hair.

Again Bo showed him the shiny metal of his hand gun. Knowing no further persuasion was required, he pointed toward the oxblood red door with a slow, arrogant smile.

"Knock," he said again, softly, almost whimsically. "I'll back you up."

Reuben crossed to the sidewalk under the awning. He glanced back once at Maggie, standing alone in the parking lot. Grimly he set his face and tapped on the door.

There was a wait. He knocked louder.

Maggie gasped as the door burst abruptly open.

A huge bearded man wearing jeans, a sleeveless t-shirt, and a leather vest grabbed Reuben by both shoulders and threw him backward into the room. Cursing and laughing the stranger waved feverishly to Bo to come in.

"Oh, man. He's on beyond stoned," Bo snarled under his breath. He pushed Maggie ahead of him. "Get in there, go on. An' don't cause no trouble, hear?"

Maggie was too frightened to cry. She stumbled into the motel room and hugged herself against the wall, not making a sound.

The slender young man they called Danny peered at Reuben and Bo through worried eyes.

"You brought a kid," he noted, seeming confused by her presence.

"Well, dog bite a biscuit!" Bo slurred sarcastically. "Danny-boy, you don't miss a trick."

"Why would you bring a kid? Here?"

Kobra, waving a liquor bottle with affected aplomb, announced, "He had the foresight to bring some entertainment for the evening. You got no imagination, Danny, that's what's wrong with you." He raised his eyebrows, smiling widely. His bleary eyes washed over the little girl's form in slow and calculating waves.

"Nobody don't need no imagination to know what's wrong with you," Bo muttered, too low for Kobra to hear. "Cops set one foot in this door, they'll have us all up for possession." He looked hiddenly out the window, holding the curtain open no more than a quarter-inch. He announced out loud, "she's our hostage, Kobra. If we get in a bad place we can trade her for freedom. So don't go messing with her."

Maggie looked warily around her. The motel room smelled of beer and cigarettes and an acrid smoke she didn't recognize. The ashtrays were overfull. There were bottles on the beds, and in the sink, and one lying broken in a puddle on the bathroom floor. The big mirror over the dresser was broken, too. Scattered across the dresser top were overturned vials of what looked like medicine or vitamins—pills of various shapes and colors. These had also spilled onto the floor.

She heard Bo demand with an obscenity, "You think this business is a bloody party or something? You think that's what this is all about?"

Kobra, their leader, laughed out loud. It was a harsh sound that made Maggie want to shrink into a tiny shadow against the wall. She looked at the floor and pretended that she wasn't there. She was home, in daylight, dragging Mama's tea strainer through the creek water, catching minnows. Jackson was with her, telling her to come home to supper.

Reuben's eyes, dark with worry, never left her face. Abruptly, he bolted into the bathroom and vomited violently. He returned rubbing his blanched, perspiring face with a towel.

"Nerves like a rabbit," Bo sneered in an undertone.

"Thought my man would be here by now," Kobra was saying. He tossed his gun onto the bed.

"Whoa—careful with that, my friend," Danny cautioned.

"You're such a girl," Kobra scoffed. "Anyhow, had to find some way to pass the time waiting on Hank. Figure a man can worry himself into an aneurism, —or—he can kick back and enjoy a good smoke!" He drew deeply on a tiny stub of hand-rolled weed. "And now we got a little sweetheart to join our party." He beckoned with both of his huge hands to Maggie. "C'mere, sugar pie. Come here and sit in my lap. Kobra's big old belly will get you warm."

Maggie simply looked at him through serious round eyes, too frightened to process his words.

Bo raised his voice. "I told you, we don't want to be bartering with damaged goods. She's just a hostage, that's all." He peered out the window. "Everything looks quiet enough. But still no sign of Hank."

"Your man ain't coming, is what I think," the quiet stranger with no name fretted, rousing himself to glare at Kobra. "I say let's get moving. We can't take a chance by waiting any longer."

The big man rolled his eyes. "Hank's bringing extra weapons, ammo, and all the money. You think we can cross the state line and hide out who knows how long on that pitiful pile of nickels and dimes and one-dollar bills that Bo and Danny brought in? Now shut up about it. You're getting on my nerves."

"He's late is all," Bo chimed in. "He'll be here. We ain't going nowhere until Hank comes, and he knows it. We can't pull this off without him."

"It isn't safe here." The nameless man looked from one to another, uneasily. He was older than the others. His face was disturbingly intense, yet without genuine expression.

Kobe belched loudly. "It's safe enough."

"Never mind the job," Reuben entreated. "Let's just get out of here, Kobe. Something's gonna go wrong, I can feel it. I'm tellin' you, man."

"My friend here ain't got no nerves for this line of business, that's what's wrong with him," Bo said with a tauntingly charming smile. "Pay him no mind."

Bo picked up the gun from the bed and held it by one finger through the guard, letting it swing idly back and forth. "Sometimes you got to wait," he murmured, his voice as smooth and sweet as vanilla pudding. "An' when you got to wait, you gotta be cool. Very—very—cool." He cocked the gun, grinning patronizingly as Reuben stiffened. Then he set the safety. "You'll learn."

Reuben cast a glance at Maggie, hugging the wall in silence. Her eyes were fixed on him.

"You all right?" he asked her.

She did not attempt a reply. She merely watched his face.

"You, little girl. Come over here an' set with me," Kobra's voice was a menacingly silvered thread interwoven in a verbal tapestry of uneasy words.

From the corner at the head of the bed, Danny moved surreptitiously closer to Reuben. Sidling close, he pretended to cough and covered his mouth. He murmured in a muted tone, "That your little girl, man?"

"Kid sister," Reuben whispered back without turning his head. His eyes were fixed watchfully on Kobra's coaxing hands.

"This ain't no place for her, man. You gotta get her out of here," Danny warned, his lips barely moving, his demeanor in no way betraying that he was having a conversation. He took a deep swig from the bottle of rum in his hand. Reuben, following his lead, lit a cigarette and hid his whispered words behind the smoke. "I can't. Bo already said he'll kill me and her both."

"Mm." The skinny young man shook his head sympathetically.

Reuben eyed the gun on the bed. He yearned to have it in his hand. But Bo's fingers were inches away from the weapon.

"You even *think* it," Danny whispered. "You'll be dead. Your little sister, too."

"Maybe that would be better in the long run," Reuben answered desperately, starting to make a move.

"Wait," Danny breathed. "I've got an idea." He moved away a little, simultaneously calling out, "Kobe, give her some of the good stuff to smoke."

"What the—?" Reuben was instantly defensive, but a quick, solemn glance from Danny silenced him.

Kobra chuckled. "That might be fun," he conceded. He said to Maggie, "Come here, sugar, you don't need to be afraid of old Kobe. You ever smoke a cigarette?"

Reuben took a step forward, but again a keen glance from Danny made him pause.

"Let her try it," he urged. "It won't kill her."

There was something in his words that Reuben recognized vaguely as a signal. He held himself in check. Danny had never caused him any harm in the joint. He wasn't known to be a trouble-maker. He had served a year for possession of marijuana. If he hadn't gotten in with Kobra and the others, he would likely have gotten his life back on track by now. Reuben decided to trust the young ex-con. Kobra laughed out loud. "Come on over here, Sugar-Pie, don't be so backwards. You're old enough to try some of this. Betcha you'll like it. Double-dog-dare you to try! Come on, be a good girl." He held out the stub, and Maggie, who was well trained to obedience, responded to his command and drew closer to him. Reuben was rigid, his jaw locked. Bo was holding his hand gun deathly still now. His eyes were two slits, piercingly fixed on Reuben's face, in undiluted threat.

Maggie took one breath from the cigarette stub that Kobra held for her, and gagged, choking feverishly on the smoke. The room filled with a cacophony of voices:

"Breathe it in, breathe it in," someone coached.

"Take it away from her, she didn't inhale, she's just wasting it."

"Here, girl, give it to me."

She looked to Reuben, her eyes blurred over with tears, gasping for breath.

"You gotta inhale, kid," someone instructed. "Try again."

"Oh, man," Danny said, swearing. His raised voice stood out over the other noises. "I forgot about — Rube, didn't you tell me she's got that bad thing wrong with her lungs?"

His eyes shot to Reuben, fraught with meaning.

"Her lungs—? Oh! I know what you mean—asth—asthma—" Reuben replied with quick understanding. He turned to Kobra. "She has asthma, man. Real bad. And we don't have her medication—I need to get her out of all this smoke, get her breathing clear!"

Kobra's grin had faded. "I never meant to—do her any harm, man. I didn't know. How bad is it?"

"It's bad. She'll likely die if I don't get her to breathing better," Reuben replied intensely, forcing himself not to look at Bo. "Right now."

"Take her outside in the fresh air," Kobe ordered with a curse. "And you—Danny—open up these windows and turn that fan on!"

Bo stood. "You never mentioned nothing to me about her havin' asthma," he accused, with obvious suspicion.

"Give her some of this whiskey," offered the man with no name. "It's good for cough."

"Not this kind of cough. Besides, she's not used to that stuff, it'll choke her worse," Reuben waved the bottle aside. "I'll take her up to the snack machines and get her a Pepsi."

"You ain't goin' nowhere, you—"

"Shut up, Bo—" Kobra roared. "Go on, Reuben, we'll get it all cleared out; y'all come on back in five-ten minutes, it'll be clear. And NO more smokin' you bunch of filthy cockroaches!" Kobe barked out commands in all directions. "Put that cigarette out, Bo!"

Gratefully, Reuben picked Maggie up in his arms and headed for the door.

He stopped suddenly, aware of a gun pressed against his rib.

"Don't go gettin' any crazy ideas, Rube. I got your car keys right here in my pocket. We're in this together. You try to hot-wire that car, you're a dead man."

"Get out of my way. I got to get the child some air."

"Let him alone, Bo!" Danny intervened. "That asthma thing can kill a person, for real."

Bo tucked his gun out of sight. "Go on," he mumbled. "But don't be gone long."

Reuben slid out the partially opened door with Maggie in his arms. The door instantly shut tight behind him.

Maggie was still coughing, but less. Reuben set her down and held her by the hand. Together they walked out into the night, into that peculiar darkness which seemed almost day, so full it was of the brightness of neon light.

Out here the air, by contrast, seemed suddenly sweet and fresh. The color returned quickly to Maggie's cheeks in two splotchy pink patches, like fever. Reuben gave her a reassuring smile. His own heart was pounding with the tangible danger still all around them.

"Do I have azma?" Maggie asked, looking up into his face.

"No, baby girl. You're gonna be just fine."

He led her, still holding her hand, in the direction of the motel office. Nearby were the drink and snack machines. Just once did Reuben risk a glance backward. Sure enough, there was a slightly widened ribbon of yellow light at the edge of the heavily curtained window in the room they had left behind. They were being carefully watched.

Reuben spoke quietly to the little girl at his side. She was clinging to his hand as if for life.

"Don't be scared, Maggie. You're gonna be okay. I'm gonna make sure you're okay."

She nodded, looking up into his face with such earnest trust in her eyes that his own eyes blurred, hot and stinging. Overwrought emotions assailed him. Fear, shame, regret. Under his breath he whispered into the night air, "God is my witness, little girl, I never meant to get you tangled up in this mess. And I'll get you safe out of it, or die tryin'."

He kept them walking at a regulated pace. Not too fast, not too slow. It was a struggle because Reuben felt on fire with fear. They reached the ice machine, the coke and snack machines. Reuben's chest was pounding. He lowered himself, sitting on his heels, to face Maggie at her level. He fought to keep his voice calm, normal.

"You hungry?" he asked Maggie. "You want something?"

She shook her head no.

Reuben studied her. Her face told him nothing. "You want a Pepsi, don't you?"

"Okay," she whispered.

He hung his head down with a sigh, seeming to look at the sidewalk beneath his feet. He rubbed one hand wearily across his eyes.

"We got to do something about you, I don't know what," he mumbled under his breath. "This ain't no place for you to be. We got to get you home somehow."

He didn't look at her. He fed coins into the drink machine and handed her a cold Pepsi, and bought one for himself. Then he put two quarters into the snack vendor and yanked one of the chrome knobs. A packet of Oreo cookies rattled into the bin.

"Take 'em," he advised. "If you ain't hungry now, you will be later."

He stood up, sucked on the Pepsi bottle and looked restlessly around the motel grounds. Through the glass windows he saw a large woman in a red dress awake in the office, watching television. Maybe she would agree to keep Maggie with her. But he knew what would happen if he opened the office door, with Bo watching from the motel room window with his loaded gun. Reuben shivered.

Maggie, trembling in her nightgown, took only a sip from her drink and set it down in the empties crate for safe-keeping.

There were piles of crates for returnable bottles. It was like a barricade. Reuben studied it, beginning to have an idea.

Although she was not hungry, the sweet white frosting in the cookies tempted Maggie, and she kept the package clutched in her hand. The two stood close together, for a brief instant, in awkward silence.

Reuben thought he would burst if he couldn't put something into words for her. Something needed to be said. But he could think of nothing. He put his hand behind her head and tousled her hair lightly, tenderly. She gave him a quizzical look.

"You should be home, little girl," he murmured. "Lining up your crazy dominoes under the window in the living room. Playing with your skinny little cat—" his throat suddenly clenched, and with effort he took another swallow of Pepsi.

There was no more time.

Maggie was turning the cellophane-wrapped package over in her hand, looking for a way to open it, when suddenly the whole world around her seemed to explode into confusion.

A black and white police car appeared from out of nowhere and spun reeling into the parking lot. Another followed and parked crossways from the first, blocking off any means of exit. The siren set up an ear-splitting wail, as bursts of red light flashed in repetitive circles against the white brick buildings.

Lights came on in motel rooms. A few doors opened and were hastily shut. A woman screamed. Policemen spilled out of the car—crouching, running. Armed.

Reuben dropped the Pepsi bottle. It shattered on the sidewalk.

"Stay right there," he shouted to Maggie, pushing her to safety behind the stacks of wooden crates. "Don't move for anything, hear?"

Like a frightened deer, Reuben sprang toward the room in which his former cell-mates were waiting.

Before he could reach it, the door of Kobra's motel room burst open, and Bo was running for the truck, cursing like a madman. He screamed something at Reuben, and then fired a wild shot toward the police car.

Everything was suddenly insane. Everyone was shouting at once, and still the siren was whining, louder than all the yelling.

A policeman crouched behind the first car leapt up, fired once at Bo, and ducked down again so quickly that his image was almost invisible to the eye.

Maggie flattened herself against the brick wall of the motel, hidden by the wooden crates and frozen with fear. She had no earthly idea what to do. A policeman with a grey moustache had somehow spotted her and was shouting something at her, waving to her to move—but Reuben had told her to stay put.

Unseen by Maggie, a highway patrol car came spinning into the parking lot of the motel. It reeled, and jerked to a stop, and Lester Burnett sprang out from the passenger's side.

Above all the noisy confusion, Maggie heard her father's clear voice, calling her name. She looked around in astonishment, saw him, and ran wildly toward him, with a single, passionate sob "—Daddy!"

The child threw herself headlong into his arms. Lester swept her up, clutching her against his heart, holding her.

"Daddy—" was all she could say, brokenly, between wrenching sobs of pent-up fear and desperate relief. She clung to him like a small child, her arms clasping his neck and her legs locked around his waist.

Lester could not speak at all. He only held onto her as if he intended never to let her go again.

Out of the motel room came Kobra, staggering, still drunken and dazed, his face in a furious frown at all the commotion. He opened his mouth like an attacked bear and roared from sheer rage, stumbling toward the red and white truck. He pushed Reuben out of his way, grabbing for the rifle behind the seat.

What happened next—how it happened—no one knew for sure.

There was a sound. A single shot. It was loud, and yet not so very loud. Hardly more than the noise of a child's pop-gun. Hardly different at all. Just a pop—sudden—over in an instant—yet the echo of it seemed to hang over the parking lot like a fog that would never roll out.

Reuben heard the shot, but could not figure out who, if anyone, had taken a bullet. Bo was staring at him—motionless, as if in shock. The bullet must have hit Bo, he reasoned. He took a step in the direction of his one-time friend, but discovered he was suddenly light-headed. Reuben stumbled slightly but managed not to fall. Yet he found himself sprawled on the black asphalt parking lot, looking up at a million sparkling stars.

It did not seem strange or troubling to him that he had fallen. The sheer beauty of the night sky astonished him. The stars, one by one, seemed to burst open, blooming into large white snowflakes of pure and gentle light. He felt the chill of seasons changing, and his body shuddered. Slowly he turned his head to see mortal men running in slow motion, shouting in muffled voices words without meaning. His eyes drooped half-closed. The pavement might have been a feather bed, it was so easy beneath him.

Reuben rolled his head to one side; the whole earth turned with him. His eyes, vaguely focusing, found the little girl, the one thing he still remembered, and he was overwhelmed with tender emotion, seeing that she was safe. What the danger had been, he couldn't recall. But it was gone now. Someone was holding the child, hugging her, and she was hugging back. Grateful tears rimmed Reuben's eyes. Joy flooded his overfull heart, surging upward, spilling into his throat. He coughed and the intensity of love poured out from his throat and chest in bright red ribbons.

Reuben's body felt curiously at rest—the long-relentless pulse hushed, blood pressure free-falling. All the while, the joy was growing within him, and peace replacing every thought and memory. His lifted the hand which he held pressed to his irregularly beating heart, observing his stained palm with wonder, for it seemed to him no time had passed since he was a little boy, finger-painting on a large paper spread out on the grass near the back porch.

His hands had been covered with red paint. It had seemed the most beautiful color he had ever seen. The pleasant memory brought a faint smile to his lips. Then the reminiscence melted into a single sense of completion. Waves of release flowed over his awareness: a bell rang, school was out. A whistle blew, no more peaches to pick today. The hammering ceased, the stairs were repaired. His work was finished for the night. He closed his eyes and allowed himself to rest in the peace that came to settle so softly upon him.

Everything was strangely quiet, now. Kobra and the nameless man had been apprehended and were sitting in the back seat of the squad car. Kobra had been tranquilized immediately. Danny and Bo submitted with no resistance to the two officers who pushed them against the motel wall, snapping hand-cuffs to their wrists.

An older officer, the one with the grey moustache, approached Lester. He gave a nod, by way of salutation. "There's some business, paperwork to be filled out —but we can attend to that later. Let's get you and your little gal home."

With a firm nod, Lester carried Maggie to the waiting patrol car.

Standing beside the vehicle was Danny, handcuffed, his arm in the grip of a large, red-haired policeman. He had begged, insisted, and worried the officer into letting him say a few words to Reuben's father.

"It's awful important, I promise," Danny had urged.

Disgruntled and impatient, the policeman allowed him his chance.

Danny forced himself to looked into Lester's face. "There's something you got to know—" he began.

Lester cut him off with contempt and anger. "Don't want to hear nothin' you have to say."

"No—please listen—I understand how you feel about all of us."

"No. You don't."

"But you have to know something. Your son Reuben didn't want to be here—"

"Well he *was* here," Lester said shortly, turning away.

"—only because Bo had him at gunpoint."

Lester paused in the act of getting into the squad car and turned with a questioning expression. He looked from Danny to the cop and back. "What are you saying?"

"Bo forced Reuben to meet up with us. He never wanted to be here. And it was Bo who brought the little girl along as a hostage—"

"That'll do," the large officer said sharply. "You've had your say. Come on."

Lester could only stare.

The policeman tugged on Danny's arm, pulling him away. The young man dragged his feet, talking faster and louder.

"—only thing Reuben had on his mind—was to get her away from this place—get her back home—safe—I swear—"

He was silenced by the policeman who gave his arm a rough jerk. "That's enough. No more stalling." He propelled Danny toward one of the squad cars, pushing him harshly into the back seat. The red-haired patrolman got in the front with his partner and the car spun out of the motel parking lot.

There was a moment of intense silence.

"What do you make of that?" Lester asked the patrolman with the grey moustache.

The older man raised his eyebrows. "The little girl was pretty well hidden from view behind those drink crates. I tried to get her to come to me, but she wouldn't."

"Reuben told me to stay," Maggie murmured without raising her head.

The two men looked at each other meaningfully. "Could be he *was* trying to protect her?" Lester wondered aloud.

The officer nodded soberly. "Could be he *did*."

"Hm," Lester agreed. Still holding tightly to his daughter, Lester climbed with care into the back seat of the black and white car.

The patrolman pulled out onto the early morning highway, taking them home.

"Mister, I know you don't care a thing about this right now, but I just want you to be aware. There was a $15,000 reward offered for information leading to the arrest of the one that called himself Kobra. He was wanted in three states. That money will come to you."

If Lester heard, he made no reply.

The first light of dawn found the Burnett family gathered in silence around the kitchen table. Only five-year-old Nathan was upstairs still asleep, oblivious to all that had transpired. Albert had retrieved his car keys and headed home, after promising Iris he would come back tomorrow.

Martha glanced into her husband's coffee cup, found it half-empty and cold, and filled it with hot coffee.

Not a word had been spoken for the better part of the past half-hour. The silence was broken only by occasional muffled sniffling from Iris, who sat with a wrinkled Kleenex at her nose. Her eyes, rimmed deep pink, glanced apologetically around the table. No other tears had been shed, and she was ashamed. She did not understand that shock had truncated their natural emotions.

Sonny sat leaning back in his chair, aimlessly turning the sugar bowl around in his hand, keenly embarrassed by the solemn silence.

Maggie sat in her father's lap, her cheek resting against his shoulder. Jackson had fetched Nellie down from the closet, and she held the doll pressed against her heart like a bandage. In her other hand she still clutched the unopened package of Oreo cookies.

Across from her, Jackson lay with his head on the table, weary but sleepless. He stared, scarcely blinking, through the window over the sink, lost in thought.

Grandma had been brought to a chair close beside Martha's. She sat patiently with her hands folded in her lap, more accustomed than the others to the face of tragedy and death.

It was Martha who spoke, finally. "Anybody else need fresh coffee?"

No one answered her.

"Yours is cold, Sonny," she said, touching the mug. "Don't you want a fresh cup?"

"Don't worry about it, Mama," he mumbled, embarrassed. "Just sit down. Nobody needs anything, okay?"

Iris tried, unsuccessfully, to stifle a sob. "I'm sorry," she lamented in a thin, strained voice, dabbing with the Kleenex. "I'm trying not—"

Lester said, "It's all right. You're all right."

Martha sat back down at the table, leaning her forehead into her hand. She spoke to her husband from her heart, as if the two of them were alone.

"What went wrong with Reuben?" she implored. "Do you know? We brought him up no different from the others. But he turned out different. And I don't know why, Les, I don't know why."

"Maybe there's no 'why' to be known," Lester sighed.

Martha shook her head vaguely. "No, Les. I'm afraid that somehow or another we failed him."

Lester nodded slowly. "It may be. But I know this. From what we've been able to learn, at the end he was trying to do good—for Maggie. Trying to protect her—and get her back home."

Martha shaded her face with her hands, sighing.

Another long silence was uneasily broken by Sonny asking,"What you gonna do with all that reward money, Daddy? You ought to spend some of it—get you a new car or something."

"I expect I'll spend all of it, in time," Lester replied quietly. "First off, I'll be paying for Reuben's funeral. His casket."

Sonny put down the sugar bowl and looked around him at the circle of faces.

"Look—now that just ain't fair," he said abruptly. "I ain't trying to be ugly or nothing, but a fact is a fact. Reuben brought this on himself. He made his own choices. It's a shame, and all that, but the plain fact is—this here was bound to happen, sooner or later."

For a stunned instant no one could do anything but stare in reply.

Then Martha stood up, steadying herself by holding onto the back of her chair.

"That may be true, son," she said, quietly. "But if you think that means there's somehow less to grieve over—well—you have a mighty lot ahead of you to learn."

For the first time since receiving the news of the shooting, Martha's eyes filled with tears. She turned her face away, maintaining her dignity, and slipped soundlessly out of the room.

Maggie began to cry.

Grandma reached out both arms, a silent offer to take her. Lester settled the child carefully in his grandmother's lap, shot a shaming glance at his eldest son, and went to look after his wife.

One by one, the others left the room.

Iris tiptoed down the stairs not long after, to find Maggie still in Mae's lap, sound asleep.

"I'll have to wake her up," she whispered regretfully. "Maybe she'll go right back to sleep. Come on, Ragamuffin. Let's go upstairs to bed. Just wake up a little."

The child's eyes opened and she slid obediently out of her grandmother's lap. She caught Iris's hand and followed her without a word.

Upstairs, Maggie put the cookies and Nellie at the foot of her bed. "Can I sleep with you?" the child begged Iris.

"Come on," her sister agreed. "Hop in."

Iris was grateful for the warm body that snuggled and wiggled its way hard against her abdomen. She would have held her even closer, if she could.

Usually the family would be getting up about now. She was grateful for sleep.

"Where is Reuben now?" Maggie asked abruptly.

Iris's heart lurched at the sound of her brother's name. She swallowed hard.

"Reuben died, honey-child."

"Is he in Heaven?"

"Yes," Iris promised her. "Go to sleep now, okay?"

"Will I ever see him again?"

"Not right away."

"When?"

"Well, when you go to heaven. No more talking."

"So is Reuben in heaven now?" Maggie persisted.

"Yes."

"How do you know?"

"I just *know*. I know because—because—the good thing Jesus did is way bigger than all the bad Reuben could've ever done."

"Oh."

"Go to sleep now, baby girl," Iris whispered.

Maggie drifted off soon after that. But Iris lay awake watching the sky lighten to a delicate rose. She felt her heart lighten, too, and realized with chills that with her own clumsily spoken words she had stumbled upon healing.

Across the long hall Martha and Lester lay awake in bed, watching the clouds flow languidly across the sky. When the clouds covered the moon, nothing could be seen in their small, spartan room. When they cleared, it was almost like daylight, because the moon was full.

Martha listened to her husband's breathing. She thought he was asleep. But when she looked, his eyes were open, staring at the ceiling, a shadow among shadows.

"Can't sleep?" Martha whispered.

He shook his head. "Feels like I may never sleep again."

She hugged him closer and stroked his bare chest with her palm.

He turned, facing her.

"You're beautiful—you know that?" he said quietly, tracing her eyebrow with the rough tip of one finger.

She smiled.

His fingers touched her hair. "Girl, you haven't even taken down your hair," he said with a smile. "Don't it hurt? Lying on those clips and pins and things?"

"I was too tired."

"Here, let me. Give me your brush."

She took it from the night stand and placed it in his hands.

Lester began gently pulling out bobbie pins and miniature combs, and the elastic band that held it all in place. He took the brush and carefully eased it through her golden-grey hair. When he was satisfied there were no tangles, he portioned her hair into three lengths and, as best he could, braided these together, fastening them awkwardly with the elastic band.

Then he laid back down and drew her into the safety of his arm. "Now maybe you can rest." He closed his eyes.

Martha was deeply touched by his kindness. Her emotions overflowed and she began to cry again.

"Honey, it's all right," Lester soothed her.

"I don't want to keep crying and crying," she managed to say.

"Cry as much as you need to. Cry it out."

Lester said no more, just patted her arm calmly, letting her weep.

The clouds covered the moonlight and for a moment the room was dark. Then it was flooded with white, milky light again.

"We been through a lot. We're gonna get through this, too," Lester promised.

Lester and Martha agreed that Maggie would be better off not going to Reuben's funeral.

At the precise moment when Reuben's body was being lowered into the ground, and Preacher Lawson was beginning the final prayer, Maggie and Jackson were sitting on the back porch steps which Reuben had repaired, debating whether or not to go down to the creek.

They were both barefoot and wearing overalls. The weather was nothing less than glorious—a riot of pure white clouds against a transparent blue sky.

Jackson had argued for twenty minutes, trying to persuade his sister to come fishing. But she was in a pensive mood, with little to say.

She had found a fine, straight piece of oak branch which she intended to keep for a walking stick. Now she sat tapping it, gently and rhythmically, against the step, her thoughts absorbed, apparently, in the sky.

Jackson spit out the gum he had been chewing too long and looked at his sister with one eye squinted against the sun.

"If you for sure don't want to fish, we could just go wading," he suggested.

"No," she said slowly. "But you go. If you want to."

Jackson shook his head. "It was just an idea."

He pulled a weed out of the grass and threw it contemptuously as far as he could toward the woods, muttering, "Dadburn dandelions. Multiply worse'n rabbits."

"They're pretty," Maggie observed.

Jackson raised a grim eyebrow. "Yeah, but what you don't know is—Mama will cook them things, the green part, and make us eat 'em. You don't want none of that, trust me."

Maggie's eyes studied her brother's face. "You serious?"

"Serious as can be."

Maggie pointed. "There's another one."

She watched her brother uproot it and send it sailing after the first.

Maggie went back to tapping her stick on the step. Her eyes wandered again to the puffs of shining clouds in the sky.

"I helped Reuben fix these stairs," she said without warning. "He let me—"

"Maggie," Jackson interrupted. "I'm supposed to be getting your mind off Reuben and the funeral. Cooperate a little, can't you?"

She said, "How come Mama said for me to stay here? I'm not scared about dying. Are you?"

"Am I what?"

"Scared to die?"

Jackson shrugged. "I reckon I'm kinda partial to living."

Maggie thought this over a minute and then resumed tapping the edge of the step with her stick.

The boy stole a look at his sister—her blue-grey eyes round and waif-like under a ragged edge of untrimmed bangs, her face pale except for a sprinkling of freckles newly discovered by the sun.

She was thin in her overalls, with her small white hands clutching the walking stick. There seemed to him something pitiful about the way she looked today. His eyes blurred a little, and he brushed them hastily with the back of his hand.

"I don't know why you won't go fishing with me," he complained irritably. "It's a fine day for it."

"You can go without me," she said again, with a shrug.

"Maybe I will."

They sat together in awkward silence for a moment.

"Jackson."

"What."

"I don't know how to think about Reuben."

"What you mean?"

"Sonny says he was bad—"

Jackson scoffed, "Like Sonny knows anything."

"But he wasn't bad to me," Maggie reasoned. "He bought me cookies I didn't even ask for." Her voice drooped. "I don't want to think bad about him."

"Then don't."

Maggie sighed. "But it's all big inside me. In my head. I have to figure something out. But I don't know exactly what."

Jackson looked at his sister's face, shielding his eyes from the brightness of the sun behind her. He had rarely heard her talk so much at one time. He wished for something wise to say, something that would take that adult expression out of her eyes. Something to bring back the child he used to watch reaching eagerly for crickets and kittens and minnows.

But this thing had left its mark on her. Nothing would ever completely erase it. He lowered his eyes, rubbed the sunshine out of them.

"Look," he told her. "I'm going to the creek and see if the fish are biting. You come on down when you get ready, hear?"

Maggie nodded.

Jackson stood. He hesitated for a moment on the step. Looking at his own feet, he spoke slowly.

"Here's what I know," he said. "What Reuben had on his mind those last few minutes before he got shot was a way to get you safe home. And those cookies, to keep you from going hungry. Sonny can talk all day long. It don't change the truth."

Maggie looked up. "Truth?"

"Reuben had good in him most people couldn't see. But you seen it. You got that to keep."

With those words, the boy picked up the long bamboo pole that served him for a fishing rod and started for the woods.

He walked without hurry, his eyes following the chipmunks as they scampered nervously out of his path.

The squirrels, from safe heights, scolded fiercely but could not turn him back.

Only when he reached the ragged green thicket and was ready to disappear into the half-hidden path did he stop. The sound of his sister's voice reached him there.

He turned.

"Wait, Jackson," the girl called. "Don't go without me. I want to come too."

"Come on then," the boy answered.

And resting the end of his fishing pole in the dry dust, he waited for her.

The End

Printed in the United States
By Bookmasters